Coral Cottage and Seabreeze Inn series

"Jan Moran is the new queen of the epic romance." —
Rebecca Forster, *USA Today* Bestselling Author

"The women are intelligent and strong. At the core is a
strong, close-knit family." — Betty's Reviews

"The characters are wonderful, and the magic of the story
draws you in." Goodreads Reviewer

The Chocolatier

"A delicious novel, makes you long for chocolate." – *Ciao
Tutti*

"Smoothly written...full of intrigue, love, secrets, and
romance." – *Lekker Lezen*

The Winemakers

"Readers will devour this page-turner as the mystery and
passions spin out." – *Library Journal*

"As she did in *Scent of Triumph*, Moran weaves knowledge of
wine and winemaking into this intense family drama." –
Booklist

The Perfumer: Scent of Triumph

"Heartbreaking, evocative, and inspiring, this book is a powerful journey." – Allison Pataki, *New York Times* Best-selling Author of *The Accidental Empress*

"A sweeping saga of one woman's journey through World War II and her unwillingness to give up even when faced with the toughest challenges." — Anita Abriel, Author of *The Light After the War*

"A captivating tale of love, determination and reinvention." — Karen Marin, Givenchy Paris

"An epic journey with the most resilient of heroines as our guide. It is a book to savor." — Samantha Vérant, Author of *Seven Letters from Paris*

"A stylish, compelling story of a family. What sets this apart is a backdrop of perfumery that suffuses the story."— Liz Trenow, *New York Times* Bestselling Author of *The Forgotten Seamstress*

"Courageous heroine, star-crossed lovers, splendid sense of time and place capturing the unease and turmoil of the 1940s; HEA." — *Heroes and Heartbreakers*

"A thoroughly engaging tale, rich in all five senses." — Michelle Gable, Author of *A Paris Apartment*

"Jan rivals Danielle Steel at her romantic best." — Allegra Jordan, Author of *The End of Innocence*

BOOKS BY JAN MORAN

Contemporary Series

Coral Cottage

Coral Cafe

Coral Holiday

Coral Weddings

Seabreeze Inn

Seabreeze Summer

Seabreeze Sunset

Seabreeze Christmas

Seabreeze Wedding

Seabreeze Book Club

Seabreeze Shores

Flawless

Beauty Mark

Runway

Essence

Style

Sparkle

20th-Century Historical

Hepburn's Necklace

The Chocolatier

The Winemakers: A Novel of Wine and Secrets

The Perfumer: Scent of Triumph

Life is a Cabernet

JAN MORAN

HOLIDAY

THE CORAL COTTAGE AT SUMMER BEACH
BOOK THREE

CORAL HOLIDAY

CORAL COTTAGE AT SUMMER BEACH, BOOK 3

JAN MORAN

SUNNY PALMS

PRESS

Library of Congress Cataloging-in-Publication Data

Moran, Jan.

/ by Jan Moran

ISBN 978-1-64778-040-1 (epub ebook)

ISBN 978-1-64778-059-3 (hardcover)

ISBN 978-1-64778-042-5 (hardcover)

ISBN 978-1-64778-060-9 (paperback)

ISBN 978-1-64778-041-8 (paperback)

ISBN 978-1-64778-044-9 (audiobook)

ISBN 978-1-64778-043-2 (large print)

Published by Sunny Palms Press. Cover design by Sleepy Fox Studios. Cover images copyright Deposit Photos.

Sunny Palms Press

9663 Santa Monica Blvd STE 1158

Beverly Hills, CA 90210 USA

www.sunnypalmspress.com

www.JanMoran.com

"The new theater production sounds fabulous," Marina said to her sister as she swept carrot scraps into her compost can in the kitchen of the Coral Cafe. Her grandmother's garden would thrive with the rich compost.

"You can read the script if you want." Kai leaned across the counter. With her glittery T-shirt of a surfing Santa Claus, Kai was already in the spirit of the coming holiday season. "What are you making?"

"Carrot cake. Brooke brought a fresh harvest from her garden this morning. I'm adding new autumn and winter dishes to the seasonal menu." Marina nodded toward a rack in the kitchen. "There are warm cranberry-orange muffins if you want one."

"Yum," Kai said, plucking one from a pan. "I have you down for the role of the mother in the play. A young mother," she added with a wink.

"Thanks for the distinction," Marina said, smiling. "But I'd rather not be on stage."

"You're kidding, right?" Kai turned on Christmas music and sat cross-legged on a bench at the chef's table, nibbling her muffin. "You were on the air every day for years, so I know it can't be stage fright."

"Reading the news before camera operators is hardly the same as performing before a live audience," Marina said.

Kai and Axe, a local construction contractor, were launching their inaugural theater production at the new Summer Beach Performing Arts Center, which they'd nicknamed the Seashell because of its curved, half-dome shape. Axe had been dreaming of developing the hillside land for an amphitheater for years.

"You performed your role as a news anchor," Kai said, sweeping her wavy strawberry blond hair into a topknot and poking a pencil from the table through it. "What's the difference?"

"I wasn't angling for laughs. You're the entertainer, not me." Her sister had been touring with a musical theater group for years before her ex-fiancé had tendered her resignation and she lost her position with the troupe. "Besides, I'm through with that on-air life."

"It's just our friends and neighbors." Kai leaned forward, her elbows resting on her jeans.

"That's even worse."

"Don't tell me you're afraid of them."

"Petrified." Marina made a face and pushed up the sleeves on her floral-print chef jacket. Even though the beach had taken on an autumnal chill, it was still warm in the kitchen.

Marina had been baking—and tasting—since early this morning. Cinnamon-dusted churros and blueberry tarts were already going fast with patrons. She might never have her sister's lean frame again, but Marina was petite, and every morsel lingered on her waistline. Still, she was so happy to be running the cafe she'd dreamed of for so long.

Kai grinned. "It's Jack, isn't it?"

Marina shot her sister a glare to quell her questions. "Who would make the picnic boxes?" This past summer, she'd made take-out boxes for customers to buy during the afternoon shows. Those shows had been to test attendance. People brought blankets to sit on and performers practiced material meant for larger venues. Marina had sold enough boxed sandwiches and sides to make it worthwhile.

"Brooke can serve the food boxes." Kai poked out her lower lip in a pout. "Come on. I haven't found anyone else to cast in your part."

"I'm sure you will. Or write her out of the musical." Marina slipped off her jacket and fanned her face.

Even though the high summer season had ended, visitors still filled the beach on sunny days. That would diminish during the coming holidays and winter, so Marina couldn't lose her focus over a holiday production.

She looked up from her work. Kai had gone uncharacteristically quiet. "And stop pouting. That hasn't worked on me since high school."

"Ha, that's what you think." Kai laughed. "Audition sign-ups start today, and you might lose the part I wrote for you. Besides, it won't be the same without you."

"Give it up, Kai. I'm far too busy." Marina turned away to wipe down the counter.

Just then, a customer with shocking pink hair and a tiny dog in a matching puppy pack waved at them from the patio. Marina nodded back. "Gilda at table number three needs her check."

"What do I charge for her Chihuahua's plate?"

"You're kidding, right? It was only three bites. Besides, Pixie always eats for free here." Grinning, Marina wound her damp rag and popped it in her sister's direction. "Get back to work."

Kai slid off the bench. "You'll be sorry," she called over her shoulder as she flounced from the kitchen.

Marina chuckled, but she was determined to stay out of the production, even though her sister had adapted the story from a beloved classic with Axe. She suspected that feelings were developing between them.

As she disinfected and wiped down the countertop, she watched Kai. Her sister hadn't seemed this happy since she'd won a part in her first touring production. And now, she was writing and planning to direct. To pique everyone's interest and entice them to attend auditions, Kai had been keeping the actual story a secret.

Tonight was the big unveiling and invitation to sign up for parts. Kai had planned on holding the event at their grandmother's Coral Cottage. When interest outgrew the venue, she shifted it to the Seabreeze Inn that their friends Ivy and Shelly ran.

Usually, Marina would do anything for Kai. But not this time.

Her reasons were none of Kai's business—although she did want to see Kai and Axe succeed.

Last spring, when Axe had built the dining patio and renovated the guest cottage on her grandmother Ginger's beach house, he'd heard Kai singing through an open window.

Kai had worked with Axe all summer on staging and promoting the new outdoor amphitheater. His construction team built a temporary stage that was little more than a platform, and audiences gathered on blankets and folding chairs to listen to local musicians and watch school drama club skits. They had productions during daylight hours because electrical was still being installed. By the end of the summer, the heavy construction began, and Axe and his team built a larger stage with professional lighting.

The first real production would be the holiday special.

Marina wrung out her cleaning rag and tossed it into a hamper destined for the laundry. When she turned around, a little boy barreled into the kitchen, followed by a lanky yellow Labrador with an awkward gait that didn't slow him down.

"Guess what?" Leo flung his arms around Marina. The ten-year-old was a replica of the man who sauntered behind him, with thick brown hair, a lean frame, and expressive eyes. "Kai asked me to audition for the holiday play. Isn't that cool?"

"Sure, if that's what you really want to do," Marina replied, leaning over to hug him.

The dog wedged its way between them, and they both laughed. Scout wagged his tail, and Marina scrubbed his neck as the playful dog planted a wet kiss on her cheek.

"It would be fun," Leo said, his eyes sparkling with excitement. "Dad is going to take me to the audition sign-ups today."

Marina saw the pride in Leo's eyes as he turned toward Jack. Only recently had Leo learned that Jack was his father. His mother hadn't told her son or Jack about their brief encounter a decade ago. While Marina respected

Vanessa's decision not to marry, she knew firsthand how difficult it was to raise children on your own. Marina still missed her husband Stan, even though he'd died twenty years ago.

Jack rested his hands on his son's shoulders. "I didn't know Leo would be so excited. Kai asked me to invite his friend, Samantha, too."

"That could be fun for them." As Marina met Jack's gaze, her heart quickened at the startling blue eyes that never failed to capture her attention.

Jack shifted on his feet, looking uncomfortable. "Would you, uh, like to join us there?"

"Hey, there's Samantha," Leo said, pointing toward his best friend on the beach. "I'll go tell her." He took off, and Scout bounded beside him.

"Is that a date?" Marina smiled at Jack and leaned against the counter, waiting for his reply. He had asked her out for dinner in the village earlier in the summer. They'd talked until the restaurant closed and shared a kiss that had warmed her to her core. But he hadn't made good on his promise to make time for her in his life and go out, which had been his idea. Still, Marina knew he was often occupied with Leo. She lifted her chin. She was busy, too.

Jack gave a nervous laugh. "Not really."

Marina raised her brow in anticipation, but Jack was silent. *Again.* Something her daughter once said popped into her mind. What was the phrase Heather used with her friends when they were in a going-nowhere relationship? *He's not that into you.*

"I can do better than that," Jack said, touching her hand.

Or was he? *Lots of mixed messages here,* she thought.

"I'm waiting," she said, teasing him. She slipped her fingers through his, enjoying the warmth of his hand and hoping for a sign from him.

"About that." Jack looked down at their clasped hands. "Between Ginger's book and Leo's school and extracurricular activities, I don't know where the hours go. I've always been a spontaneous kind of guy, so maybe we'll go out soon."

"Life is busy," she said lightly, trying to hide her disappointment. This wasn't the first time she'd heard that excuse.

The tightness around Jack's eyes relaxed. "I knew you'd understand."

She was trying, but she needed more than this. While Jack had awakened the desire to have a real relationship in her life, he wasn't following through.

Heather's words hovered like a cartoon bubble over his head. *Just not that into you.* Maybe he liked to flirt but had no intention of following through. She'd known men like that. While it could be fun, harmless banter, her heart had become too involved.

She tried again. With a playful smile, she asked, "So, shall we book the next opening on your action-packed schedule?"

Shifting, Jack averted his gaze toward Leo. "I really can't commit to you right now."

Marina swallowed her pride and inclined her head toward Leo. "Right. So, the usual for you two, or shall I add another ice cream for Samantha?"

Jack squeezed her hand before letting go and whistling to Leo. He cupped his hands like a megaphone and yelled, "Ask Samantha about ice cream." He waved at the girl's parents, Denise and John, who had recently bought a home in the village and were long-time friends of Leo's mother. They nodded their approval.

With a small sigh, Marina turned to start a fresh pot of coffee for Jack. He brought Leo here almost every day after school. Jack would have coffee—light, no sugar—and Leo would have an ice cream sundae. He was spoiling the boy, but Jack hadn't been in his father role long enough to realize that.

He leaned across the counter. "Everything about my life in Summer Beach is new. I'll try to get better at juggling so we can spend more time together. Just the two of us. But right now is kind of a tough time to commit to anything. Maybe next year will be better."

"You know where I'll be." Marina smiled, though her heart sank at his words. They were forming a bond—she and Jack and Leo—though she almost wished they wouldn't come to the cafe so much. Perhaps she was expecting too much of Jack, and he was becoming too comfortable in their easy, friendly roles.

Unless this is the way he wanted it. If so, she wished he'd cut the charade of a possible romance and let her go.

The two children raced to the cafe. Scout had run straight into the waves lapping the shore, and now his fur flung droplets as he ran beside them.

"Samantha wants a hot fudge sundae, too," Leo said, catching his breath. "And she wants to audition with me."

"That's great," Jack said, giving Leo a high-five. "Go grab a table for us."

The two children dashed onto the patio, where a few other customers in beachwear lingered over fruit smooth-ies. After they sat down, Scout flopped by their feet. His tongue lolled to one side in what looked like a lopsided grin.

Two young women at a nearby table reached out to rub Scout's neck. That dog and its owner sure could melt hearts.

Marina turned back to Jack. Maybe friendship was all he wanted. She had been satisfied with that for years when the twins were young, but now, she was ready for a relationship. If she had any courage at all, she should ask him right now and get it over with.

Just as she opened her mouth to speak, a torrent of staccato yaps exploded on the patio, followed by deep barks.

"Oh, my gosh, Pixie and Scout are getting into it," Marina cried, tearing from the kitchen. Jack flew right behind her.

Pixie had escaped Gilda's backpack and was running circles around Scout, who looked bewildered for a moment before deciding the Chihuahua wanted to play. Leaping around Pixie, Scout slid into a bistro table, toppling it. The potted aloe vera plant Marina had placed on the table crashed to the deck.

"Scout, wrong!" Marina cried, lunging to protect another teetering table and plant.

Jack tackled Scout, who squirmed in his arms, still eager to play with the enchanting little Pixie.

Gilda scooped up the Chihuahua and hugged her tightly. "Naughty, naughty girl." She spoke in a loving singsong tone and smothered Pixie with kisses.

"Well, that's a mixed message if I ever saw one," Marina said as she picked up a table. *Sort of like Jack.*

"I have to put Scout into an obedience training class," Jack said, looking contrite.

Marina pressed the shocked succulent back into its pot and dusted her hands. "I think Pixie started it."

Gilda blushed. "She can be a little tease, dancing around dogs. But at least we have her kleptomania under control. Mummy takes her to counseling every week, don't I, baby-kins?" Gilda kissed Pixie again before stuffing her wriggly form into the puppy backpack she carried.

Marina could only shake her head. "It's all over, and I have sundaes to make."

"Yay," Leo and Samantha cried, clapping.

Marina returned to the kitchen. After washing her hands, she brought out bowls for ice cream. From the corner of her eye, she saw Jack sit on the bench at the chef's table. He seemed embarrassed over Scout's display. She poured a glass of water for him and slid it across the counter.

"Thanks," Jack said, drinking deeply. "So, do you still plan to serve boxed dinners at the theater?"

A safe topic, Marina thought. "That business was pretty good in the summer, so it should help us through the slower winter season. Ivy and Shelly also asked if I could prepare boxed spa lunches for the wellness weeks they're planning at the inn."

"The key is to attract people to Summer Beach in the off-season," Jack said, rubbing the day-old scruff on his chin. "Ivy's art show and your Taste of Summer Beach both did well."

During the Scout and Pixie bout, Marina had lost her nerve to ask him the question that had been keeping her up at night. She had never been great at idle chit-chat, and he seemed to be skirting a topic, but she could hardly look away from him. Intelligence shone in his eyes, and she longed for a deeper connection with him.

The truth was, she was afraid to hear his answer. "And how is your book writing?" she asked instead, wincing inside at her lack of originality.

"Your grandmother has quite a lot of stories," Jack replied. "The publisher just ordered another book in the series, so I'm working on a new round of illustrations. Never thought I'd be living in Summer Beach with a son and a house and a dog—let alone spending my time sketching and editing children's stories."

"It's a long way from fancy Pulitzer prizes."

Jack frowned at that. "I never asked for that recognition. Those honors are earned, and I could have easily lost my life for that story."

Having worked as an investigative journalist until the sabbatical he'd taken in Summer Beach, Jack was no stranger to hazardous situations. A thought occurred to Marina. "Do you miss developing important stories?"

Jack dismissed the idea with a slight wave of his hand, though a shadow crossed his face. "I've already done that, and I turned down the last assignment offered to me. It's all about Leo now. Vanessa's health is improving, but I'm still trying to do as much for Leo as she'll let me. Between Leo's school, homework, and sports, it's quite a lot."

The coffee maker sputtered to an end, and Marina brought out a cup, thinking as she reached for the pot. Young Leo was the product of a desperate one-night stand on a dangerous assignment. Vanessa hadn't shared the boy's existence with Jack until she suffered a serious health scare and began to put her affairs in order. Even Jack admitted that he hadn't been attractive husband or father material back then, and Vanessa didn't want to marry anyway. Marina had to admire the woman's strength and foresight to provide for her son.

As she poured coffee for Jack, she tried to read the look in his eyes. Was it disappointment or regret over leaving a high-powered career? Or, maybe the demands of sudden parenthood were overwhelming him. Whatever it was, he looked haggard.

With a grateful grin, he lifted the cup to his mouth and sipped. "Nectar of the gods. I don't know what I'd do without you."

Marina tilted her head. "What do you mean by that?"

"Coming here with Leo is the bright spot in my day." Jack touched her hand again, smoothing his fingers over hers. "We're good friends, Marina. I feel like I can ask you anything. You make this inept new dad look good in Vanessa's eyes. She's trusting me more with Leo, and that's thanks to you."

Good friends. His choice of words stung her, though she tried not to let it show. Jack really didn't know what he wanted. If only she could control the way her chest tightened whenever he was around.

"I've nurtured my share of bruises, sunburns, and broken hearts for my kids," she said lightly. "You'll get the hang of it before long."

She slipped her hand from under his and hurried to the pantry for hot fudge and chopped nuts.

When she returned, Jack frowned. "You seemed sort of abrupt just then. Is everything okay?"

Marina twisted her mouth to one side as she heated hot fudge in a small saucepan over a burner. "We're both busy, and I understand the demands you're facing. You'll get through this." She opened the freezer.

"With you," he added, holding her gaze. "You don't know how much our talks mean to me."

"You'll always find me right here behind the counter."

Was he just here for coffee with a side of parental advice? Marina shoved a scoop into a container of vanilla ice cream. She plopped generous servings into two bowls and drizzled hot fudge over them.

Jack watched her. "Leo likes extra nuts."

She added whipped cream and chopped almonds, and she topped the sundaes with fresh cherries.

"I'll take these out to them," Marina said, slipping from the kitchen. Kai had already left to prepare for her event.

Clutching his coffee, Jack followed her.

After serving the children, Marina tidied a few tables before making her way back to the kitchen. Her grandmother, the incomparable Ginger Delavie, was in the kitchen sorting through tea bags. She had put on a kettle and brought out two of her favorite cups. With her imperious posture and perennial can-do attitude, Ginger exuded an air of capability. The Coral Cafe existed only because she'd encouraged Marina to take over the old guest cottage.

"Jack and Leo have become quite the regulars," Ginger said, nodding toward their table. "But he's spoiling the boy with those sundaes every day."

"Leo plays a lot of sports. He burns it off."

After selecting an assortment of tea, Ginger lowered her voice. "Anything interesting with Jack to report?"

Feeling frustrated, Marina shook her head. She could feel heat flushing her cheeks.

"I'm not being nosy, but I am looking out for you,"

Ginger said. "After that dreadful Grady, it's clear that you
need a second opinion. As for Jack—"

"Our relationship just fizzled out," Marina said,
although she appreciated Ginger's concern. After their
parents died, her grandmother had always looked after her
and her sisters with utmost love and care.

"I'm sorry," Ginger said, crestfallen. "I honestly thought
Jack was better than that." She smoothed a manicured
hand over her russet-colored hair, freshly cut and tinted at
the village salon. "Still, look at that as a test run, my dear."
She paused. "Jack is a brilliant collaborator, by the way.
This will be a marvelous series of books. I hope you won't
feel too awkward around him."

"I'll be okay. He must be working hard on them."

Arching an eyebrow, her grandmother nodded sagely.
"Did he ever ask you out?"

Marina shook her head. "He just called me a 'good
friend' and told me how much he values my parenting
advice." She flipped a hand over her shoulder. *Was he really
that dense?*

Ginger touched her shoulder. "Good friends sometimes
turn into more."

"Not this time," Marina said. "Earlier, I thought we had
more between us." As she put away her ingredients, she
wondered if a few kisses counted as *more* to men like Jack
who'd traveled the world and had probably known count-
less women. Maybe a few kisses didn't mean anything
to him.

"He needs to settle into his new role and station in life,"
Ginger said, looking thoughtful.

Marina could tell her grandmother hated to give up
hope. "So, are you saying I should wait for him?"

"That was an impartial observance, my dear. Don't extrapolate to find the answer you want. I'm not usually wrong, but I could be this time. You must let Jack go. Remember, life has a way of working out—but only if you work at it." Just then, the tea kettle whistled, and Ginger waved at another older woman who appeared at the entry to the patio. "Perfect timing. There's my friend. We're having tea before Kai's big announcement party. What fun that will be. I'll go with Maeve, but I'll see you there."

"I'm not going."

Ginger raised her brow in surprise. "Just because your sister acts confident, don't think she doesn't need the support of her family. This is her first show at a new theater, and it will benefit all of Summer Beach. You're not busy, so put up your closed sign and join us for an hour." She straightened the collar of her starched plaid shirt.

Marina smiled. Even in her casual pressed jeans, Ginger was a force. "I'll think about it."

"That sounds like a *no*."

Marina hugged her grandmother. "Don't extrapolate, Ginger."

Just then, a tall, well-built man strolled onto the patio dining area. Glancing at him, Marina said, "See, I have to stay. I have another customer." She picked up a menu and made her way to greet him.

"Welcome to the Coral Cafe," Marina said, gesturing toward a prime spot near Ginger. "This table has the best ocean view."

"Looks like they all do. What a beautiful location." He looked at her curiously and hesitated. "Excuse me. You're Marina, aren't you?"

"Do I know you?"

"You might not remember me, but I was Stan's friend. We served in Afghanistan together."

Memories of evening card parties and laughter surged through her mind. "Is that you, Cole?"

A smile lit his weathered face. "That's right. I didn't know you had a cafe. Last I heard you were serving up the daily news in San Francisco. This is quite a change."

"Sometimes life throws us a curve," Marina said. Although his face had aged and a thin scar slashed one eyebrow, Cole Beaufort was still as attractive and fit as he'd always been. He and Stan had been very close.

"I've thought of you often," he said, taking a step toward her. "You caught a bad break with Stan. I still miss the guy. How are your twins—Heather and Ethan, right?"

Marina was pleased that he'd remembered them. "Heather is in college nearby, and Ethan is pursuing a career in golf. He wants to turn pro. And what about your family?"

"My girls are fine. Helen is in college, and Deborah just got engaged. She wants to make me a young grandfather." He shook his head. "Are we really getting that old?"

Marina laughed. "You still look good, Cole. And how is Babs—is she here with you?"

"We didn't make it," Cole said, his dark brown eyes softening at the memory. "My deployments didn't help. Babs got lonely and disgruntled, and I can't blame her. After the divorce, she married a good man. Another Marine, retired like me now." Cole pulled out a chair for her. "Can you sit with me for a few minutes? I'd sure like to catch up."

Marina glanced around the patio. Other guests had left, and the only tables filled were Jack's and Ginger's.

Her grandmother could help herself in the kitchen, and Jack wouldn't be needing anything else. She saw him glance her way, taking casual interest in this friendly newcomer.

So did Ginger.

"I'd like that," she said. "Let me know what I can get you, too."

"A cup of coffee if you have it. I'm not that hungry. After creeping out of Los Angeles in the slowest traffic I've ever seen, I need to revive myself, stretch my legs, and get a view of the ocean."

"Coming right up." Marina hurried to the kitchen. A few minutes later, she returned with two cups and a plate of cinnamon-dusted churros she'd made that morning. Ginger was talking to Cole, who had stood to speak with her.

"Once a Marine, always a Marine," Ginger said, her voice rich with approval. "And a good friend of Stan's, who was a marvelous soul. I'm so glad you came to visit."

"As luck would have it," Cole replied. "Are you sure you and your friend wouldn't like to join us?"

"Thank you, but you and Marina probably have a lot to catch up on. It was very nice to meet you." Ginger turned to Marina, and with a slight lift of her brow, conveyed her approval before returning to her friend.

Cole's eyes lit at Marina's tray. "I haven't had churros in years. Didn't you used to make these?"

"I did. For our card parties." She placed a steaming, beach-themed mug before him and the churros between them.

"Stan was an ace at poker." Cole chuckled at the memory.

"It seemed like he was good at everything."

"Not the least of which was choosing his mate," Cole said, catching her eye.

Marina smiled at the compliment. "Are you staying in Summer Beach or passing through?"

"I planned to peel off at a pretty little lake just south of here and drop my pole, maybe catch a few fish. I brought my camper and thought I'd knock around for a couple of days. I have a few bungalows that I fixed up and rent out, so my time is pretty flexible."

Marina glanced at what Cole called a camper. As usual, Cole was being modest. A sleek luxury motorcoach that probably cost as much as a home was pulled along one side of the street. The silver and blue metallic paint sparkled in the sunlight.

She sipped her coffee, thinking about the nice life he enjoyed, and she was happy for him. "Why don't you stay in Summer Beach a few days? I can cook for you again—like old times."

Cole shook his head. "You do plenty of cooking. Let me take you out tonight. We still have a lot to talk about."

Marina hesitated, smiling at the idea.

"I don't mean to be presumptuous," Cole quickly added. "If there's someone else…"

"No, there's no one in my life." Feeling Jack's gaze on her, Marina glanced at Ginger, who nodded her assent. Her grandmother would look after the cafe tonight. "I'd like that, thank you."

Cole had always held a special place in her heart, and he'd been a good friend to Stan. They chatted a little more until Ginger and her friend rose.

Her grandmother paused by their table, checking her watch. "Just look at the time already. Perhaps Cole would like to join us at Kai's holiday kick-off. Marina's sister and a partner are opening a new amphitheater in Summer Beach. We're all supporting her."

"Well, I don't know if Cole—"

"I'd like that," Cole said. "We have to support our family's efforts."

"That's exactly what I said," Ginger replied. "I'll put up the *Closed until Dinner* sign. I'm going with my friend, but you and Cole can meet us there."

Across the patio, Jack and Leo and Samantha left their table, too.

Marina lifted her hand and waved to Jack. Although he noticed, he gave her only the briefest of nods.

Ginger noticed Jack's curt dismissal, too. She pressed her lips together in what Marina recognized as displeasure.

That was it. As much as Marina cared for Jack, she had to relinquish him. The fledgling relationship they had wasn't going anywhere. Words without action grew stale.

"I'll finish here and join you in a moment," Marina said to Cole. She glanced at his motor home. "I have a smaller car we can take."

Cole jerked a thumb toward his sleek craft. "On longer trips, I hitch my car to the back, but I didn't think I'd be treating a lovely woman tonight."

Marina laughed. "It's just dinner." But as she looked into Cole's warm brown eyes, she noticed the interest in his gaze.

She picked up Jack's coffee cup and the children's dirtied ice cream dishes and whisked them to the kitchen sink.

Marina hurried through the back door of the main cottage and climbed the creaky wooden stairs to her old childhood bedroom just past Kai and Brooke's rooms. After removing her chef's jacket, she slipped on a lightweight cashmere sweater in soft shell-pink over her dark denim jeans. Ginger had given her the sweater a couple of Christmases ago.

She wanted to look decent for Cole—but only because they were going out to dinner afterward. He'd been Stan's good friend, after all. After changing her shoes by the old iron bed, she added a fresh spritz of lemon verbena *eau de toilette* to mask the *eau de café* odor that clung to her skin.

Smoothing her reddish-brown hair in the mirror, she thought about what Ginger had said and smiled at her reflection. Maybe life did have a way of working out.

2

When Marina parked in front of the Seabreeze Inn, Kai was outside talking to Ivy Bay, the proprietor, and welcoming others who were arriving.

"Go into the ballroom," Kai said, directing people. "Axe will check you in."

Cole unwound his long frame from the passenger side of Marina's turquoise Mini-Cooper. They made their way past swaying palm trees and up the stone steps of the old beachside inn.

"And who do we have here?" Kai asked, her curiosity clearly piqued.

"This is Cole, an old friend," Marina replied. "He and Stan served together in Afghanistan."

Kai tapped a finger on her chin. "You have excellent presence. I'm sure we can find a part for you."

Chuckling, Cole put up his hands. "I'm not auditioning. Marina and I are going to dinner tonight."

"Ginger asked that we come to support you," Marina said quickly. "Cole is just passing through."

"If you change your mind, this is a great place to live," Kai said. "Some say, 'Life is better in Summer Beach.' We've been visiting since we were little, and I always wanted to return." She flicked a look at Marina. "Maybe you will, too, Cole."

"My sister is always kidding," Marina interjected. "Let's go inside."

"Wow, would you look at this?" Cole stepped across the threshold, pausing to admire the grand Spanish Colonial architecture of the old beach house.

As Kai followed him in, she whispered to Marina, "Just trying to help. He's really good-looking."

"Shh. I don't need your help."

"I guess not," Kai said with a wink. "Jack's loss."

"Cole is an old friend." Marina stepped inside next to Cole. Yet, there was something solid and reassuring about him.

Kai and Ivy's sister Shelly had become friends, and they had volunteered the ballroom at the inn for rehearsals.

"What an incredible place this is," Cole said.

"It has quite a history," Marina said. "My grandmother knew the original owner, Amelia Erickson, although she says she's still not at liberty to talk about her."

A look of interest lit Cole's face. "I'm not sure I follow that."

"This house has a lot of mystery surrounding it," Marina explained. "Our grandfather was a career diplomat, and Ginger had a fascinating career in government as well. She has a lot of stories—some she can tell and some she can't since they're still classified."

"Her stories shift like the sand anyway," Kai said.

That was true, although Marina suspected that wasn't due to memory impairment but to Ginger's creative streak. She simply liked to entertain people. Likely, Ginger had been privy to many State secrets, just as her husband Bertrand had been. Perhaps that was her way to keep people guessing—or entertained.

"Come in," Axe bellowed, waving them into the chandelier-studded ballroom where holiday carols were playing in the background. He was a broad-shouldered man with sandy hair, a rich baritone voice, and a friendly manner. His Montana cowboy boots added height to his already towering frame.

As Marina strolled across the wooden parquet floor honeyed with age, the kitten heels she'd hastily changed into tapped beside Cole's Italian loafers.

An interesting choice for a fishing trip, she thought, glancing at his shoes. But he probably had room for an extensive wardrobe in that rolling palace.

Ivy and Shelly's niece, Poppy, was hanging the last of a row of stockings over a large fireplace that anchored the grand room. Everywhere Marina looked, vintage Christmas ornaments they'd discovered at the inn last year glistened, nestled among fir branches that filled the room with a wintry holiday aroma. Although Summer Beach wasn't as cool this time of year as what she was accustomed to in San Francisco, she appreciated the spirit.

"Hi, Marina," Poppy said, swinging her silky blond hair over a shoulder. "It's so good to see you."

Marina introduced Cole. "He's an old friend of the family," she said, deciding that sounded appropriate.

"It's nice to meet you," Poppy said. "In a few weeks,

we'll put up the Christmas tree, a menorah, and a kinara. We'll host festivities for Christmas and the Festival of Lights for our guests who visit for this season of thanks and cele- bration. Our doors are open to anyone who wants to come."

Marina glanced at Cole and hesitated, but only for a moment. "If you're here, maybe you'd like to join in."

"I'd like that," he said, touching her shoulder in a friendly manner. "This is what I miss about small towns. I grew up in a farming community in the Central Valley of California. My kids don't like to go back—they usually spend Christmas with Babs. A lot of the people I knew moved away, so the town isn't the same anymore."

"Then this would be fun for you," Marina said.

Cole smiled. "I'm awfully glad I ran into you. This was unexpected, but it's so nice of you to include me."

"You were like family, Cole. And you always will be." Marina could relax with him. He and Stan had looked after their young wives with such love and care. Marina recalled when she and Babs had become pregnant with their first children at the same time. But then, Stan didn't return from Afghanistan, and Cole was still deployed there. Marina returned to live with Ginger and give birth to the twins. She blinked at the memories.

Having Cole here was like having a piece of Stan back in her life. She'd missed that.

Near the fireplace, Kai was conferring with Axe. Nodding, she turned toward the gathering crowd and passed out a stack of papers. Marina took one and passed it on to Leilani and Roy Miyake, owners of the Hidden Garden nursery, where she bought plants for their garden and the dining patio.

Next to them sat Darla, an older woman who lived next door to the inn. Her royal blue hair and rhinestone-studded visor were her trademarks, along with her slightly gruff personality.

A minute later, Marina's sister Brooke rushed in, her Birkenstocks slapping on the hardwood floor. Ginger motioned to her to join her.

Jack was already there with Leo and Samantha. After a brief nod to him, Marina tried not to look in his direction, although she could still feel a magnetic connection between them.

Marina sighed. These feelings had to stop. There was little chance of a future with Jack. Why couldn't he have simply asked her out and made his intentions clear? They could have settled their attraction for each other one way or another, instead of this infuriating limbo they found themselves in. Or, maybe she should have asked him out, but she had an old-school attitude about that. Instead of chastising herself, she turned her attention back to Kai and Axe.

After the room had filled, Axe began. "This is the official unveiling of our new holiday program for the Summer Beach Performing Arts Center, also known as the Seashell, cowritten by yours truly and the incomparable Kai Moore —with special posthumous thanks to Charles Dickens. And now, I'm turning it over to Kai to tell you about the production."

A cheer went up through the crowd.

"Woo-hoo!" Shelly called out from the entrance to the room.

Kai laughed and went on. "Many of you have been asking about our new show, and now I can finally reveal it. Drum roll, please!"

Laughing, people drummed their hands on armchairs and tables. Marina was so proud of her sister. She caught Ginger's gaze from across the room and nodded, glad that she'd come after all. While she'd been grumpy over Jack earlier, that was no reason to withhold support from Kai.

Yesterday, she'd overheard Kai ask Jack to audition for the play—that was why she didn't want anything to do with it. But Summer Beach was her town, too. And it had been long before Jack Ventana ever arrived with his silly old Volkswagen van and nutty dog.

Although she really loved Scout. Marina bit her lip and looked at Kai.

A smile wreathed Kai's face. "Axe and I have adapted an old book into a musical, and we've added a beach theme. It's called, 'A Christmas Carol...at the Beach.' You probably know the story about Ebenezer Scrooge and the three ghosts of Christmas. There are a few other parts, and we need a crew and other volunteers. We've made a list of roles, and you can sign up for those that interest you. Auditions start tomorrow at Ginger Delavie's Coral Cottage on the beach. A map is on the back if you need it."

"I have to warn you all," Axe added. "Competition will be brutal, so bring your best game. Not all the parts require singing, but a few do. We have a couple of very special coaches for that."

"I'll be your director, so I'm here to help." Kai bobbed a little curtsy, and then she held out a hand toward the doorway. "And you'll receive special instruction from a VIP benefactor who knows a thing or two about singing, too. She's our very own Christmas Carol—Carol Reston, that is."

The Grammy Award-winning singer and Summer

Beach resident stepped out from behind Shelly and waved. Carol's curly henna hair was piled onto her head, adding height to her petite frame. Her voice was the soundtrack to so many lives here. Marina had grown up dancing to Carol's love songs on the radio.

"This will be a fabulous show," Carol said. "I can't wait to work with our cast and crew."

Applause rolled across the room, and soon everyone was chatting about what they wanted to do.

"Are you trying out for a part?" Cole asked.

"I don't have time," Marina said.

Standing nearby, Kai overheard her. "We're going to need a lot of extras, too. You could do that. Low commitment there. Come on, Marina."

"We'll see." Only if Jack isn't involved, Marina decided, although she didn't say anything.

"I'll wear you down yet," Kai said.

Cole chuckled. "Your sister sounds as persistent as you, Marina." He tapped his temple. "I haven't forgotten about how you used to play cards."

Marina laughed. "Maybe I'll challenge you again."

"Maybe you will," Cole said.

Something about the way he said that caught her attention. Was there more than friendship in his feelings for her?

"Let me know when you'd like to leave for dinner," Cole said.

Marina picked up her purse. "I'm ready."

She knew life could change in an instant. But her heart, not so much. Determined not to glance back at Jack, she tucked her hand into the crook of Cole's arm to leave.

3

*W*ith the refrigerator door open, Jack turned to Leo. His son was doing his math homework at the kitchen table in their cottage near the beach. Through open windows, the rhythmic sound of ocean waves and fresh breezes lifted Jack's spirits. "Pizza or hamburgers tonight?"

Leo looked up and made a face. "Hey, Dad, I saw this cooking show on TV. They made some cool stuff like Aunt Denise does. I can help if you want to try."

"I thought kids didn't like the fancy stuff," Jack said.

"Only some things. I'm getting tired of pizza."

"Said no kid ever," Jack replied, laughing. "How about chicken nuggets?"

Leo put his pencil down. "I'm not like every other kid. You know I like a lot of different things, right?"

Jack was desperately trying to figure out everything about Leo, but Vanessa had a ten-year head start, and he was playing catchup. Plus, his skills were limited. "Okay, burgers it is."

"Could we go to the Coral Cafe?" Leo kicked his wooden chair leg. "I like seeing Marina."

"About that. Maybe I overdid it with the sundaes." And perhaps he underdid it with Marina. Silently, Jack chastised himself for missing out. He'd been too distracted and too slow. And now this guy Cole had stepped into his place. Not that Jack had any claim on Marina, but he hadn't counted on feeling this way without her. "We're going to take a break from the Coral Cafe."

"That's okay." Leo shrugged. "Hot fudge sundaes are good, just not every day. Mom says they're special rewards. Like for when I get an A in math."

"Which it sounds like you will after Ginger gave you those tips. It's nice of her to volunteer in the math program at school. You be sure to thank her."

"I do, Dad." Leo squirmed in his seat. "I'm hungry. Rosa makes good salmon tacos. Mom says they're organic, too. Since she can eat more now, we get tacos at Rosa's food truck in the village. She said Rosa makes fresh food with a lot of good vegetables."

"And you like your vegetables, don't you?" The kid could eat a tomato like an apple. He had to hand it to Vanessa; she had done a great job in raising the boy. Jack shouldn't mess that up now.

Leo nodded. "Could we grow some funny-shaped tomatoes like Marina does? They're my favorites. She calls them hair loons."

"Heirloom," Jack said, correcting his son with a chuckle. "We used to grow them on the farm when I was your age. And I planted those for Marina and Ginger after Scout destroyed the garden." He shut the refrigerator and pocketed his house keys. "We can do better than chicken nuggets. Let's go to Rosa's. It's going to get chilly when the sun sets, so grab your jacket." He whistled for Scout, who loped toward them from his bed in the corner.

With the sound of the surf behind them, Jack and Leo walked the few short blocks to the village and stood in line at the popular food truck. Scout stayed close to them.

Upon arriving in Summer Beach, Jack quickly learned that Rosa and her family had been serving fresh Mexican fare to locals for three generations, and another was already in training. Casual food this good was a real treat. He missed the street food in New York, where he could walk out of his apartment and pick up a delicious hot bratwurst at midnight from a corner vendor. Even on a cold, snowy night.

Still, the choice of freshly grilled fish with organic, home-grown lettuce, cabbage, tomatoes, carrots, and onions was probably better for him and Leo. And the homemade corn tortillas and spicy jalapeño salsa were tasty.

When Jack's stomach rumbled, Leo laughed. Jack pressed his hand against his belly, which had grown flatter since moving here. Trying to keep up with Mayor Bennett on the beach, he'd become leaner and gained muscle. He felt healthier in Summer Beach, more like the laid-back kid on a farm in Texas he'd once been.

Jack chewed the inside of his mouth. He still craved a cigarette occasionally, but he'd succumbed only once after a couple of martinis with an old buddy from New York who'd passed through town. Still, when he thought about Marina, the craving grew stronger. That was a sign of frustration, and he wasn't sure what to do about it.

After ordering and getting their tacos and chilled horchata drinks with vanilla and cinnamon, Jack led Leo to a bench with a view of Main Street on one side and the ocean on the other. Sitting down, he breathed in bracing sea breezes. The sun was setting, casting golden rays across the waves and lighting the sky with coral hues. Scout panted at his feet.

"This is the life, Leo," Jack said, sweeping his hand across the scene. "Couple of guys, great tacos, a pretty good dog, and the beach. What more do we need?" He scooped jalapeño salsa onto his tacos and added more hot sauce. He liked the fiery flavor—the hotter, the better—although he might pay for it later.

"Hey, there's Marina," Leo said. He waved across the street. "Hi, Marina!"

Jack looked up. Marina was going into a restaurant with the man she was with at the inn. "Shh," Jack said.

Leo frowned. "Why? She's our friend."

"Well, yeah, but…" Jack didn't have a good answer. "She's on a date. People like privacy."

Marina turned around. "Hi, Leo." She smiled and waved, and then her date opened the door to Beaches for her. Although Jack hadn't eaten there, it was known as the finest—and most romantic—restaurant in Summer Beach.

Scout's ears perked up, and he whined at Jack. "Stay, boy." Even his dog wanted to hang out with Marina.

"Is she dating that guy?" Leo sounded worried.

"Looks like it." Jack didn't know how to talk about relationships with Leo, and he wondered how much his son knew about that.

A sad look washed across Leo's face. "I guess that's okay, because you told me that Marina isn't your girlfriend." Leo stared at his taco. "I wish she was, though. You should ask her on a date, Dad. I think she'd like that."

Jack nearly choked on his horchata. "Maybe I will."

"That would be cool," Leo said. "If she was your girl-friend, we could see her all the time. And you could get married."

Even Scout looked up with his silly, lopsided grin.

Jack felt outnumbered. Why had he been such an idiot? He prided himself on following through on what mattered. He was usually great at noting important details, getting a story straight, and lining up sources and interviews.

Yet, for all his success in investigative journalism, he'd been a lousy boyfriend. Plenty of women had told him so. Vanessa hadn't even been interested in him beyond that one furtive evening when they'd thumbed their noses at death.

"Maybe I need boyfriend lessons," he mumbled to himself.

Leo giggled. "Me, too."

Not out loud. Jack felt like smacking himself. Living alone for so long, he had a habit of mumbling to himself. He hadn't even realized it until Leo began catching him at it.

"Guess we both do," Jack said. Ready or not, it looked like he was about to face that topic with Leo.

Leo turned his face up to Jack. "Where do we go to take lessons?"

"I'm not sure," Jack said with a laugh.

"I'll look it up online," Leo said, grabbing Jack's phone beside them. He pressed a button and spoke into the phone. "Look up: how to be a good boyfriend."

"Wait a minute…"

His son stared at the screen and wrinkled his brow. "Dad, what's an—" He stopped and sounded out the unknown word. "Aphrodisiac? Did I say that right?"

"That's an adult word," Jack cried, snatching the phone

from the boy's hand. "We'll talk about that later. In a few years. Eat your taco."

"Did I say something wrong?"

"Just forget that. All of that, including Marina."

"Why?"

"It's complicated," Jack said with a sigh. So was parenting.

"I could help you uncomplicated it." Leo brightened. "I could ask her on a date for you. That's what my friend did."

"Wait a minute—you're dating?" Jack fumbled his plate, and a taco slid off.

Scout leapt to his feet, intercepting the taco in mid-air with the skill of a professional football player.

"Scout, no!" Jack dove for him, but Scout dodged him with his prize.

"My friend is. But he's older. He's twelve."

"Twelve?" Jack squeaked. He picked himself up from the pavement. Forget boyfriend lessons; he needed dad lessons. *Right away.*

Scout crunched the taco and swallowed it, but a moment later, he started shaking his head. He backed up, pawed at his mouth, and began to howl.

Jack threw up his hands, "I tried to stop you, old boy."

"What's wrong with Scout, Dad?" Leo asked, alarmed.

"That taco was pretty spicy." Jack held out the horchata. "Have a drink, boy."

Scout growled and barked at him, backing farther away. People in the village began to turn in their direction.

"Settle down, Scout." Jack reached for him, but Scout kept barking and backing away. He lunged for him, but Scout slipped from his grasp and bounded toward the restaurant.

Standing outside, Scout pawed at the door, barking.

With his heart in his throat, Jack raced after him. He knew where the dog was headed, and he had to stop him.

Just then, a patron opened the door, and Scout charged inside.

4

*W*ith Cole's hand resting lightly on her shoulder, Marina walked into Beaches. His simple touch filled her with a sense of security. She'd always felt comfortable with Cole. While he was certainly attractive, she hadn't given him much notice long ago because she was madly in love with Stan.

Now, having Cole here brought back so many shared memories. It was like going home to a safer time and place before her world had exploded. More than that, Cole was a Marine. Next to his solid, imposing stature, she felt safe and protected.

Cole gestured toward the wide expanse of windows that were rimmed with festive garlands and red holly berries. "We have front row seats to the sunset."

"It's beautiful," Marina said. With plate glass windows that framed the beach, the view was a prime attraction at Beaches. The restaurant had an excellent reputation for its menu, too. The chef had entered Marina's Taste of

Summer Beach cook-off in the summer, and Marina had been impressed with the shrimp Provençal.

She gave the maître d' her name and glanced into the open kitchen. "Is Chef Marguerite here?"

"I'll let her know you're here."

Moments later, a stout woman bustled from the kitchen. "Marina, is that you? Welcome to my restaurant."

"I've been wanting to visit for a while, but the cafe keeps me busy." Marina introduced Cole.

"I'm so pleased to meet you," Marguerite said. "Russell, our maître d', will take good care of you." She lifted her chin toward her employee. "A prime table for them, please."

Russell showed them to a table overlooking the beach where waves raced onto the shore and tumbled over rocks, sending up a frothy spray. With the sunset casting a glow around them, and candles flickering on the table, Marina thought it was one of the most romantic settings she'd ever seen in Summer Beach. Or anywhere.

As they were looking at the menu, Chef Marguerite sent a bottle of Bordeaux to the table. A waiter opened it and poured two glasses for them.

"This was a wonderful choice, Cole. How did you know about Beaches?"

"I was talking to the mayor at the inn. He mentioned it as being a Summer Beach favorite. Bennett seems like a nice guy."

Marina smiled. "He is. He and my friend Ivy just married this summer."

"No kidding?" A smile grew on Cole's face, and he leaned in. Lifting his glass to her, he said, "I guess it's never too late to try again."

Marina's neck grew warm at his comment, but she couldn't resist the question in her mind. After all, they were friends. She tapped her glass to his. "Have you tried again?"

"Not really. After the divorce, I was pretty broken up. A few friends set me up with some nice women, but they weren't Babs. I never realized the little problems we had would have erupted into what they did. I lost the love of my life, but that's history now." Cole glanced to one side, seemingly embarrassed by what he'd just revealed. "Anyway, by the time I realized I wasn't going to find a woman just like her, they had moved on, and I was out of friends."

"I can understand that." Marina's heart went out to him. He had lost someone he'd loved very much. It seemed like such a shame, but she supposed it was too late now.

Cole swirled his wine and sipped it. "I found it takes a long time to get to know someone."

"It sure does," Marina said. She thought about Grady, her ex-fiancé. How little she'd known his true nature. When a news reporter gleefully delivered news of Grady's other engagement on the air to a much younger celebrity, Marina had a melt-down on camera. That had cost her a long-term news anchor position as well as her dignity. The future she'd been planning for them disappeared in a flash.

Cole's eyes crinkled, lifting into a smile. "Trying to meet someone to spend the rest of my life with seemed like an impossible task, so I let it go. My kids and my work keep me busy enough, and I take off on trips whenever I can. If another relationship is meant to be, I think the opportunity will present itself."

"That's what I tell myself, too," Marina said. This time, her thoughts turned to Jack. Chances were growing slimmer with him. While she wasn't in a hurry, neither did she want to be ignored and strung along.

"What about you?" Cole asked. "Anyone special in your life?"

She tucked her hair behind an ear, stalling for a moment. Cole didn't want to hear about her failures in love. Instead, she gave him an easy, nonchalant smile. "Heather and Ethan take up a lot of my time, too." Although after they'd moved away, she found herself a little lonely on her own.

Cole pressed a finger against his lips in thought. "Did I hear something about you and an architect in San Francisco?"

With horror, Marina realized he must have seen the meme that zinged around the internet of her reaction to Grady's engagement. She'd managed to catch her heel on her chair, accidentally throwing herself to the floor. Not the most graceful exit she'd ever had. If only that clip hadn't repeatedly played on a continuous loop with a laugh track to millions on social media and late-night talk shows. She sighed.

"We weren't well suited to each other after all," Marina said lightly, hoping the candlelight would mask her reddened cheeks. She lifted the wine to her lips.

Yet, from the corner of her eye, she saw a flash of fur.

Like a bolt of yellow lightning, Scout charged into the dining room and leapt onto her, wide-eyed with fright and whining in anguish.

"No! Down, Scout!" Marina's chair tipped back, and she landed on the floor with Scout sprawled over her, nestling into her as if he were scared out of his wits. Wine sloshed over them in an arc, and the woman at the neighboring table screamed.

Cole jumped up. "What the heck?" In a swift movement, he dragged Scout off by the scruff with one hand and helped Marina with the other.

Jack appeared behind him. "Let go of my dog."

Scout cried and pawed Marina while waiters frantically raced after still-flaming candles rolling across the wooden floor.

"He doesn't want you," Marina said, reaching for Scout as her mothering instinct kicked in. "Cole, it's okay to let him go. Something's wrong with him."

Scout pawing his mouth as if something was causing him pain.

Marina knelt and hugged the whimpering dog to her chest. They were both covered in red wine, so it hardly mattered. "What's wrong, poor boy?"

Jack ran a hand through his hair, seemingly embarrassed. "He needs water. A lot of it, probably."

"Cole, would you hand me my glass?" He did, and Marina held the glass to Scout's mouth. The dog eagerly lapped it. "What happened to him?"

Jack shifted from one foot to another. "He ate a taco with a lot of spicy salsa and hot sauce on it."

"You fed him a taco?" Marina glared at Jack. "That's not dog food. What kind of an imbecile are you?"

Leo appeared beside Jack, panting. "It was a mistake," he said, tears springing to his eyes.

"I'll say." Leo had more compassion than Jack. Tamping down her anger, Marina cradled Scout's head in her arms and pressed the water glass to his snout again. The poor dog couldn't get enough water.

A couple at the table next to them who had just finished their main course left abruptly. The maître d' hurried to Marina. "Excuse me, ma'am, but we can't let you stay here with this dog. Even though you're friends with the chef."

"We're going," Jack said, reaching for Scout. "I'll take care of him."

"No, he can come home with me," Marina snapped. "You don't know how to take care of a dog, let alone a—" She cut herself off before she said something she'd regret.

"I'll drive you," Cole said evenly, taking charge. "We'll put the dog in the back, or you can hold him."

Leo's lip quivered, and he began to cry. "It wasn't Scout's fault. He didn't know what he was doing. Don't take him away."

Marina held a hand to Leo, and he flung his arms around her and Scout.

"Don't punish him," Leo cried.

"I only want to make sure he's okay," Marina said, smoothing Leo's hair and wiping his cheeks. She felt terrible for him. What was Jack thinking?

Leo sniffed and drew his hand over his eyes. "Can I go with you, too?"

The maître d' threw up his hands in exasperation, and Cole turned back to Marina. "We can fit the boy in as well." He held his hands out to them. "But we should leave now."

"Leo stays with me," Jack said through gritted teeth. He reached for his son and took his hand.

"Let's all go in peace," Cole said, holding up a palm. He helped Marina with Scout to the door.

Marina led Scout out. Once they were outside, the dog calmed down and slunk back to Jack.

"Hey, I'm sorry, boy," Jack said, rubbing Scout's neck. "You were too fast for me. But I'll go easy on the hot sauce from now on."

"You'd better," Marina said. Standing on the sidewalk in front of the restaurant, she crossed her arms. Jack was a disaster. How could she have ever thought she might have something in common with this overgrown man-child? "And don't even think of giving him chocolate, alcohol, or onions."

Jack scowled at her. "Do you take me for a complete idiot?"

"You don't want me to answer that." Marina pressed her lips together in disgust. "You or Leo can find a list of problematic foods for dogs online in about three seconds. I suggest you do it for Scout."

"I'm perfectly capable of looking after Scout and Leo," Jack said with a scowl. "Come on, guys. Let's walk home."

"Dad, I'm still hungry." Leo pointed at the tacos he'd left behind on the bench. A tabby cat was dragging a piece of fish from the taco.

"I'll clean that up," Jack said. "And we'll get another order to go."

While Jack disposed of Leo's food, Marina knelt and said goodbye to Leo. "You call me or your mother if there's anything you need. Promise?" She kissed his cheek.

"I promise."

Jack called back to him. "Leo, come with me."

As Leo trotted after his father, Marina watched him go. The boy looked sad, and it broke her heart. At least he had Vanessa.

"Are you okay?" Cole asked.

Marina nodded and took Cole's steady arm. This was

the type of man she should be considering. "I just didn't expect that. Would you like to return to the restaurant?"

"Another day," he said. He gestured toward her cashmere sweater. "You might want to change right away."

Marina looked down. Red wine stained the shell-pink fibers, and dirty paw imprints were smeared on the front. "I'm such a mess. My life isn't always like this, I promise."

Cole chuckled. "I'm sure it isn't. I remember you as being smart and well-organized. Come on, I'll drive you back. While you change, I can make a mean grilled cheese sandwich in the old camper for you."

"That's kind of you, but come back to the cottage with me. I'll change, and we can cook together in the kitchen. Ginger might be there, and I'm sure she'd like to hear this story. And she has an incredible wine cellar. Will you sleep in your motorcoach tonight?"

"If it's all right to leave it where it is."

"I'm sure it will be." She smiled. "And I'll drive. I don't know if you'd fit behind the wheel of the Mini-Cooper."

5

"*A*nother slice of frittata, Cole?" Using Ginger's silver serving spatula, Marina lifted a savory portion with sautéed squash and onions. They sat at the vintage red Formica table in Ginger's kitchen with the morning sun streaming through.

Last night after they returned to the cottage, Marina had prepared her gourmet grilled cheese sandwiches made with Havarti, Fontina, and Gruyère cheeses on pesto-slathered sourdough bread with thinly sliced tomatoes and green onions from the garden. After spending the evening catching up and laughing, Cole had slept in his motorcoach.

"Don't mind if I do," Cole replied. "The eggs are delicious, and this sure beats cooking box food in the camper."

"That looks pretty comfortable," Marina said, nodding toward the sleek motorcoach parked outside. It was easily the size of the tour buses entertainers used.

"It's nice enough for a bachelor, and it gives me the freedom to go almost anywhere I can drive." Between bites, he added, "I visit my children and friends—mostly Marines from the old days when I can find them."

Marina sipped her coffee, pleased that he was enjoying her food. "You sound like you have a good life, Cole. I'm happy for you."

"It is, and I know I'm fortunate. Still, it can get lonely." He took a breath as if to ask a question, but took another bite instead.

Ginger walked into the kitchen, filling the awkward moment. "How nice to have a man in the house," she said, smiling. "After you finish that sumptuous breakfast my granddaughter made for you, I was wondering if you could spare a little time to help me around the house? I have a few items on my honey-do list but no honey to do them. And Kai is holding auditions here later."

Cole laughed. "I'd be happy to help."

Marina noticed that Ginger wore her work clothes—or her version of work clothes. Pressed dark blue jeans, a navy-and-white plaid shirt, and high-topped camel trainers. With discreet pearl earrings and a jaunty cotton scarf at her neck, Ginger always managed to look chic, even when she planned to work around the house or in the garden. They could all take a few lessons from their grandmother.

Marina seemed to have only two style speeds—her conservative suits she'd had to wear on the air and her old beachwear.

"I'm surprised Kai hasn't been downstairs yet," Marina said. "Especially with rehearsals beginning this afternoon."

"She left early this morning to meet someone at the theater," Ginger said. "I saw her on my way to my meditation hike on the ridgetop. She left even before Brooke arrived to pick up your bread and muffins for the farmers market."

Cole looked impressed. "Lifelong fitness is important."

"Since you're in such fine shape, you can help me in the garden," Ginger said to Cole. "Unless you have something better to do, although I can't imagine what if you plan to keep enjoying Marina's fresh garden fare."

Marina chuckled while the tips of Cole's ears turned pink.

"No, ma'am. I'd be honored to help you as soon as I clean up the breakfast dishes."

"I appreciate the offer, but you don't have to do that," Marina said. Still, Cole was quick to disagree. She liked that about him.

After Cole finished eating, he washed the breakfast dishes while Marina relaxed, and she was impressed with his efficiency. She knew that was part of his Marine training, and it reminded her of Stan. Cole was nice to have around, and she enjoyed talking about old times with him. She didn't have many friends from those days.

"I have almost everything in the living room waiting," Ginger said.

"What did you have in mind?" Marina asked.

Ginger's eyes lit with a smile. "Besides those light bulbs in the ceiling I can never reach, I thought we should help inspire the people who are auditioning today. While I usually wait until a little later to decorate for the holidays, I decided we should start earlier. This way," she said, motioning toward the front rooms.

Her grandmother had already brought out decorations while Marina was making breakfast. "We have a few more boxes in the storeroom," Ginger said. "Cole, be a dear and help me with those."

"I'll put away the dishes and join you in a moment," Marina said, picking up the utensils Cole had washed. He followed Ginger to the storage area.

Marina had to hand it to Ginger. She knew her grandmother's holiday decorating usually took a few days, but it would go much faster with Cole and his efficient execution. They might even have it done by the time auditions began, although Marina also had to tend to lunch customers.

Fortunately, Brooke was now managing the farmers market stall. Every Saturday morning, her sister picked up Marina's baked goods and added her freshly harvested organic produce. Brooke enjoyed overseeing their booth, and it gave her a break from her husband Chip and their three rowdy boys.

After Brooke had fled the house this past summer in frustration over what she called their wild dog pack, she had reached an agreement with Chip that he and the boys would clean the house on Saturday morning while she was at the farmers market, in addition to completing other chores. So far, it was working for them.

Along with the part-timer Marina had hired, having Brooke manage the farmers market stall gave Marina more time to have a balanced life, especially on the weekends.

The manager of the market, Cookie O'Toole, had told her that Brooke was a natural. Her sister was sharing recipes and gardening tips, and she'd been selling out of her organic vegetables. She was moving more of Marina's bread, cookies, and tarts, too. With her calming, earth mother personality, people trusted Brooke and her advice.

When she talked about the health benefits of broccoli and fiber, people listened.

Marina was pleased to help Brooke, and it gave her more time off. After the summer rush, she had also started closing on Mondays. Getting the cafe up and running had been hard work, and she was relieved to regain some balance in her life.

After tidying the kitchen, Marina joined Cole and Ginger in the living room.

"That's almost everything," Ginger said, surveying the stacks of boxes.

Cole raised his brow. "If there's more, I can do that, too."

"The exterior decorations are in the storage shed," Ginger said. "We'll tackle those next. I can't tell you how much I appreciate this."

Marina laughed. "Cole, are you having regrets about stopping for coffee at the Coral Cafe yet?"

Grinning, Cole said, "Not at all. In fact, I think it was a stroke of luck that I landed here."

A smile played on Ginger's face. "Are you sure it was luck and not part of a reconnaissance mission?"

This time, Cole's ears flushed a deeper shade of pink. "I admit that I did read a review of the Coral Cafe online. And I might've seen that my old friend Marina Moore was running it. But I really did plan to go fishing."

Marina opened her mouth in astonishment. "How did you know that, Ginger?"

Her grandmother merely shrugged. "Sometimes things are too much of a coincidence. After calculating the odds, it's a simple process of elimination of alternative theories to arrive at an educated supposition. I tested my theory, and Cole just proved it. Therefore, the case is closed."

Now Cole's cheeks were turning red. "I thought it would be nice to reconnect with your granddaughter, ma'am." Cole's voice held a new level of respect.

Satisfied, Ginger nodded. "And do call me Ginger. I'll have you know, not much escapes me. But you're such a dear young man that I'll forgive you." Inclining her head toward Marina, she said, "Besides, I can hardly blame you. She's lovely, isn't she?"

"I'm standing right here," Marina said, putting a hand on her hip and only partly amused. Ginger could sometimes embarrass people with her directness.

"Of course you are, dear." Her grandmother motioned toward a tall hutch. "Would you take the other end of that garland with Cole and drape it over that piece?"

Before Marina could ask more questions of Cole, Ginger put a classic Bing Crosby Christmas album on her vintage turntable and went on directing decoration placement. Despite the sweet sound of "White Christmas," Marina couldn't help wondering why Cole hadn't mentioned that he'd planned to visit her in Summer Beach. And why did he act like it was a chance meeting?

However, one look at Ginger's satisfied expression answered her questions. Cole was lonely. He'd said so himself. Ginger must have known that he would like decorating with them, too, as he was clearly enjoying himself.

"When you're through with that, the Christmas tree topiaries go on either side of the fireplace," Ginger said. "And another pair by the front door."

Marina set to work with Cole, and before long, they were laughing together as they placed decorations around the rooms. Most of the pieces she recalled from childhood, and they gave her a warm feeling of remembrance. Some had been gifts from her parents before they'd died in the auto accident that dreadful night. Marina lifted an old-fashioned St. Nicolas that her mother had made. Smiling, she put it in a place of honor on the dining room table.

Next came more forest-green garlands, intricately embroidered stockings, and exquisite handblown glass ornaments Ginger and Bertrand had collected throughout Europe. Every ornament held a story, and Marina loved to hear them—even if the stories changed slightly from time to time.

Marina lifted an edge of a garland and draped it over the mantle. "How is that, Ginger?"

Just then, the front door opened. "To the left, to the left," Kai sang out, flinging out splayed jazz hands. "Just wait until you see how many people have signed up to audition. We're going to have a full house this afternoon." She glanced around. "Wow, just look at these decorations—they sure will help people get in character."

"Don't just stand there," Marina said with cheerful admonishment. "Give us a hand."

After seeing Kai's enthusiasm—and the community's excitement yesterday—a warm, happy sense filled Marina. This year, she would be surrounded by family and new friends; it would be the merriest Christmas she'd known in years.

Marina glanced at Cole, wondering if he might return for the holidays, too. However, at that thought, a churning feeling wound through her. She'd thought she would be spending the holidays with Jack and Leo, but with their relationship in limbo, that didn't seem like such a sure thing.

Still, she had enjoyed choosing special gifts for Leo, although she had yet to buy anything for Jack. That was just as well.

"Where would you like Mr. and Mrs. Claus?" Kai asked, pulling a pair of hand-sewn and stuffed characters from a storage box.

"Nestled on the sofa, please," Ginger replied.

Marina opened another box. "And the holiday candles?"

"Arrange those on any surface you can find," Ginger replied. "A cluster on the dining room table always looks nice. Put the silver menorah there, too, and add fresh candles to the shopping list. We're going to host many friends this holiday season." She turned to Cole. "While the girls are unpacking in here, we can bring out the exterior decorations."

"Don't forget the Santa surfboard," Kai said, unwrapping a vintage snow globe of the North Pole.

"I'd almost forgotten about that," Marina said. "We painted an old surfboard when we were kids. I didn't know you still had that."

"You haven't been back here for Christmas in a while," Kai said pointedly.

When Cole drew his eyebrows together in question, Ginger explained. "It was easier for me to visit Marina and her children in San Francisco. Kai was always here on her holiday break from the touring company."

"I often went to San Francisco, too," Kai said. "I love seeing the decorations at Union Square and the St. Francis Hotel. And the shopping is wonderful. San Francisco is magical during the holidays."

"Do you miss the city?" Cole asked Marina.

"A little," Marina replied. "It was home for many years, but being with my family is a treat."

"This will be such a happy year with the entire family in town," Ginger said. "Now, let's see to that Santa surfboard." Ginger led Cole outside to the storage shed.

While they were gone, Kai turned to Marina. "I'm impressed. I left you at the cafe yesterday, and you had a date two hours later. I think you beat my record. Where in the world did you find that handsome new boyfriend?"

As she placed candles on the table, Marina laughed. "He's hardly my boyfriend—he's an old friend of Stan's."

"If he's not your boyfriend, you should tell Jack that. You should have seen the way he was checking out Cole during the meeting yesterday."

"Was it that obvious?"

"I wasn't the only one who noticed. And then there was the fight they had over you at Beaches."

"What? Where did you hear that nonsense?"

"Shelly told me that Mitch overheard the story this morning at Java Beach from someone who was having dinner there." Kai's eyes widened. "Were you really thrown out?"

"It was nothing like that," Marina snapped, trying to untangle ribbons in another box. She jerked a couple of ribbons and tossed them back in frustration.

"Hey, don't take it out on the messenger—or the decorations."

Marina sighed. "It was Scout." She perched on the edge of a slipcovered sofa and told Kai what had really happened.

"So Jack and Cole weren't fighting over you?" Kai asked, disappointed.

"Hardly," Marina said. "Besides, Jack hasn't asked me out since summer."

"I thought the two of you were doing well after your Taste of Summer Beach event."

"So did I," Marina said. "I understand he has a lot of responsibility with Leo—plus, a new home and Ginger's book projects. But I really thought we had something special developing."

Kai unwrapped a snowman. "He still comes to the cafe a lot."

"Usually with Leo. I'm not sure what to think—or how long I should wait for him." Marina hooked glittery candy canes on the chandelier. "He sure knows what he wants in other parts of his life. You don't win a Pulitzer prize unless you know how to go after a goal."

"You're the one who tells me that matters of the heart are different." After placing the snowman beside a jeweled topiary, Kai threw a look at her sister. "And now Cole is complicating your feelings, right?"

"He's such a nice guy," Marina said. "Stan always thought highly of him." She paused. "He'd probably even approve."

Just then, the door opened, and Ginger motioned toward the lawn. "Cole is such a treasure," she announced, admiring his quick handiwork on the porch and lawn. "We'll finish the exterior decorations while Kai is holding auditions."

As Marina tidied the living and dining rooms, Kai rearranged the furniture. Marina would have to leave to begin the prep work in her cafe for the lunch crowd. Outside, a late-model truck pulled to the curb.

"Axe is here," Marina said as she stacked empty boxes

in the adjoining hallway. Ginger could have Cole move them later.

Kai's eyes lit with anticipation. She picked up a notebook she'd brought and hurried to the door. Marina had never seen her sister so happy. She was doing what she loved, and she and Axe were growing closer.

While Kai waited for Axe, she turned to Marina. "Are you sure you won't think about joining the play?" She sounded hopeful. "I understand you're busy, but I'd love for you to be a part of this. You could be an extra; that's a low-time commitment. And it's will be so much fun."

Marina knew having family involved would mean a lot to Kai. If their positions were reversed, she'd want her sisters there, too. She smiled. "Okay, count me in."

Kai bounced on her toes and threw her arms around Marina. "I'm so happy. I promise you won't be sorry. You'll have fun at the rehearsals, and then there's opening night, the nightly shows, and the wrap party."

Axe's cowboy boots thudded on the front porch, and Kai opened the door. He wore a plaid shirt and western-cut denim jeans with a vest that bore the emblem of his company, Woodson Construction.

"Everything is ready," Kai said, greeting her partner in the new theater. "I'm glad you made it."

"I just got off of a new job site, but my crew has everything under control." Axe glanced around. "These decorations look amazing. This will get people in the spirit."

"That's the idea." Kai sat at the dining room table and tapped her notebook. "I made notes about who is trying out for each part. The most important parts are old Mr. Scrooge, his employee Bob Cratchit, and the three ghosts—

past, present, and future. And Cratchit's family—especially Tiny Tim."

Axe eased his large frame beside her. "Do you have any preferences on actors?"

Kai beamed at him. "Leo would make a great Tiny Tim."

"He sure seems eager," Axe said. "Do you have the schedule for today?"

Kai opened her notebook. "Right here." She glanced through the window. "Looks like our first two are here. Leo and Jack. And I see another couple arriving. It's going to be a busy day. Shall we start with Jack or Leo?"

Marina snapped around. "Jack is really auditioning?"

"For the part of Bob Cratchit," Kai said. "Won't he be perfect? He was in the drama club in high school and college, so I'll bet he has some acting chops hidden underneath that serious writerly exterior."

Immediately, Marina wished she could take back the promise she'd just made to Kai. How was she going to face Jack every day?

6

*T*oday, Kai was posting the results of the auditions on a community bulletin board at the cafe entry, so Marina expected a crowd at the cafe.

Wearing a glittery red sweater and waving a list, Kai made her way across the dining patio. "The results are in."

As her sister tacked the list on the board, Marina tried to peer over her shoulder, but Kai had a height advantage. She had been humming "Rudolph the Red-Nosed Reindeer" all morning, and her soundtrack was still stuck on that tune.

"The decision was pretty close for some parts," Kai said. "Who knew we had so many talented actors and singers in Summer Beach?" She stepped aside with a flourish. "Ta-da!"

Marina leaned in. There, by the part of poor overworked Bob Cratchit, was the name she dreaded.

Jack Ventana.

How would she treat him now that they weren't dating?

It dawned on her that he might be uncomfortable, too. Especially since Cole had volunteered as an extra.

Ginger had given Cole permission to park his motor-coach on the property as long as he needed, although Cole found an RV park nearby.

For that, Marina was relieved. Although he was a great friend, she didn't mind a little distance. She thought about the old adage of absence making the heart grow fonder. If only she could banish Jack from her heart to open the way for a good man like Cole.

Kai was staring at her. "Well? What do you think?"

"What a cast," Marina said, trying to sound upbeat.

"Can you believe I'm singing in a scene preceding Carol Reston? I'm practically her opening act. And wait until you hear Axe in his numbers. He sounds incredible." Kai let out a little squeal of excitement. "This is going to be amazing."

"Sure will be." Jack had time for a holiday musical, but he couldn't spare an evening for a dinner alone with her? This was too much.

With a heavy heart, Marina took another look at the post.

A Christmas Carol…At the Beach
Casting Announcement
Narrator – Ginger Delavie
Ebenezer Scrooge – Axe Woodson
Bob Cratchit – Jack Ventana
Scrooge's Nephew Fred – Mitch Kline
Emily Cratchit (Bob's wife) – Leilani Miyake
Tiny Tim (the Cratchit's son) – Leo Ventana

Ghosts of Christmas Past - Kai Moore
Ghost of Christmas Present – Carol Reston
Ghost of Christmas Future – Brother Rip
Extras – Children
Logan Rushmore, Samantha Davis
Alder, Rowan, and Oakley Gardner
Estelle Garcia's Summer Beach Elementary School
Drama Club
Extras – Adults
Marina Moore, Brooke Gardner, Shelly Bay, Cookie
O'Toole, Roy Miyake, Nan Ainsworth, Arthur Ainsworth,
Flint Bay, Cole Beaufort
Others roped in as needed.

Marina spied Brooke's name. "Who's going to handle sales of the picnic boxes?"

"Brooke volunteered Chip to handle onsite sales," Kai replied. "But I understand if you need her for the cafe. I imagine most people will collect their picnic boxes before the show like they did this summer." Her sister grinned. "Brooke is sure taking charge these days."

"With that houseful of raging testosterone, she has to, or she'll get run over again," Marina said. "I'm glad to see that Chip is finally acting like a dad and not one of the boys."

Kai folded her arms. "If he does, he knows Brooke will head right back here."

People began arriving at the cafe to check the casting announcement, so Marina returned to the kitchen. She didn't want to hear Jack's congratulations.

As she put a pot of pumpkin bisque she'd made on a burner, an uncomfortable thought struck her. Maybe she was acting Scrooge-like. Although she wasn't happy with the cavalier way Jack had been treating her after professing his attraction to her, she had to admit he was talented.

Jack was an excellent writer, and Kai and Axe were probably lucky to have him in the show. Marina blew out a breath. Sometimes it was hard to remember that forgiveness and giving thanks were part of the holiday celebrations. If she didn't adjust her attitude, she'd have a lousy holiday.

But it sure was hard. Her heart still did flip-flops whenever Jack was around.

She reached for a loaf of sunflower seed and cracked wheat bread she'd made and began to slice it for today's special—the turkey with cranberry sauce sandwiches she'd created for her seasonal menu.

Cole's voice floated to her. "Hey, congratulations."

Marina smiled. "Am I glad to see you." She meant it, too. She had to get Jack out of her mind, and Cole was just the one to do it.

"How about we celebrate our off-Broadway extra debuts?"

"That sounds like fun," Marina said. "What did you have in mind?"

"How about a campfire dinner? I'll cook this time." He chuckled. "I don't think we'll be welcome at Beaches for a while."

"That's okay. I've been to plenty of fancy places in San Francisco over the years, but it's been ages since I've had supper by a campfire."

"We'll take the camper," Cole said. "It has everything we could need."

Brooke hurried into the kitchen and deposited a bag of vegetables by the sink. "Am I too late? I got to talking to Cookie O'Toole out there. She's pretty excited about the holiday show. Everyone is." She flipped her braids back. "I'm glad you called me in to help. There's a huge crowd here checking the list and talking about the show. Kai will be busy out there for a while."

"Glad you could make it." Marina turned to her younger sister. Kai has been filling in to wait tables all summer, but she wouldn't have time anymore. Heather wanted to pick up hours during her winter break from school, but her time was limited until final exams were over.

Marina introduced her to Cole. Brooke greeted him and picked up a pad to write orders. "Besides the pumpkin bisque and the turkey sandwiches, do you have any other seasonal specials?"

"Sweet potato fries with garlic aioli," Marina said. "I'm planning recipes with winter squash, broccoli, and Brussel sprouts. Your fresh produce is excellent."

Brooke grinned with pride and sailed onto the dining patio.

"You have an incredible family," Cole said.

Marina brought the turkey she'd roasted and sliced from the refrigerator. "They were my rock after Stan died. The twins were a handful, even if I hadn't been grieving. I don't know what I would have done without Ginger."

Cole glanced back at the patio. "Looks like you'll be busy today. Let me know if you need any help. I'm pretty good at carrying food to tables—that's a food runner, right?"

"Sure is, and I appreciate that," Marina said. "You might get drafted."

"I'll join your unit voluntarily," he said with a wink.

"Oh, I didn't mean the pun," Marina said, feeling herself flush at his reply. The U.S. military hadn't drafted people in years, but she still recalled her parents talking about it. "Why don't you go and meet your fellow cast members? We can catch up later."

As Cole strode away, Marina had to admire his confidence. At the front, she saw him greet Axe, who had joined Kai in welcoming their new cast members.

Ginger joined the crowd, congratulating Leilani and Roy, who had brought a velvety-red poinsettia for the cafe. Nan Ainsworth, who worked at City Hall and owned Antique Times on Main Street, was there with her husband, Arthur. Even Darla was there to check out the list and congratulate everyone. Today, a smile replaced her usually crotchety demeanor.

Before long, Marina spied Jack and Leo, along with his friends, Samantha and Logan. The children looked excited, and everyone was congratulating them, along with Jack.

As they should, Marina told herself, trying to put aside her feelings for him. She lifted her chin. Maybe she would congratulate him, too, just to prove how magnanimous she was.

"Order in," Brooke called out, clipping a piece of paper to a round metal ticket holder above Marina's counter. She snapped her fingers. "Earth to Marina. People are waiting." Brooke bustled away to another table.

Marina didn't have time to think about Jack. She checked the order before taking the sweet potatoes she'd sliced and prepped from the refrigerator.

Yet, when she turned around, she came face to face with Jack. At once, her bravado evaporated, and she bobbled the dish, accidentally dumping the sweet potatoes down his chest.

"What are you doing in here?" Marina cried.

"Sorry, I didn't mean to alarm you." He knelt to pick up raw sweet potatoes scattered on the floor.

Marina threw up a hand in frustration. "What did you do, sprint over here? I just saw you arrive."

A hint of a smile curved a corner of Jack's mouth. "This is my order, I'll bet."

"Then you'll just have to wait." Exasperated, Marina blew a wisp of hair from her face. "Now I'll have to prepare more fries."

"Give me a potato peeler, and I'll wash up."

"I can't let you do that."

"And why not? Those are my fries. We could even apply the two-second rule. A little floor dust doesn't faze me, not when you've been where I've been."

Marina glared at him. "First, it's because I serve them with the skin on. And second, because you're impossible." She leaned to one side to see out on the patio. "I hope you have Scout on a leash today."

"He's at the groomers," Jack said. A smile twitched his lips. "His fur was splashed with a lot of red wine. I tried to hose him off at the house, but he thought it was a game and kept biting the hose. Leo and I ended up more soaked than he was." He gave an exaggerated sigh. "That's the last time I take him to Beaches for dinner."

Despite Jack's ridiculous comment, Marina couldn't help laughing at the image in her mind. "I have more sweet potatoes in the cupboard. You can scrub them, and I'll slice.

I don't trust you with a mandoline slicer. And then you have to get out of here to let me work."

Brooke rushed in with another order and snapped it to the ticket holder before returning to the patio. As she and Jack fell into a rhythm, Marina caught a glimpse of Cole watching them with hooded eyes.

Suddenly, she realized she might have a problem developing.

7

*W*hen Jack arrived at the Seabreeze Inn, Kai was passing out scripts to the new cast that had gathered in the ballroom.

"Welcome, thespians," Kai said. "Here's our script for the holiday show. Once you're seated, we'll read through it so you can all mark your parts." She handed one to Jack and another one to Leo.

"Hey, Dad, let's sit up front," Leo said, scrambling to a chair on the front row.

Jack eased into one beside him. He glanced around to see if Marina was there and nodded to Leilani and Roy, who'd helped him replant Ginger's garden when Scout dug it up. Nan and Arthur were there from Antique Times, where he'd bought a kitchen table and chairs for his rental house near the beach. He smiled and waved at them.

The scene reminded Jack of his drama club days in college. He'd enjoyed that, and he had even considered a career as a playwright or actor. In the end, journalism and the quest for truth appealed to him, but he'd never lost his appreciation of the stage and the relationship with the audience.

"Best seats in the house," Jack said, ruffling Leo's hair. He was glad they were both involved in the holiday show. Vanessa usually rested in the afternoons, so Jack crafted illustrations for Ginger's books in the morning and planned activities with Leo after school.

He opened the script and flipped to Leo's part. "Here's where your part begins, son."

"Thanks, Dad."

"You'll make a great Tiny Tim." Jack put his arm around the boy. His role as a father was still so new to him that every time he uttered the word *son* or heard Leo say *Dad*, his heart swelled with love. He wondered if it would always be like that.

While people found their seats, Jack scanned the part of Bob Cratchit, the overworked and underappreciated employee of legendary tightwad Ebenezer Scrooge.

A Christmas Carol…at the Beach was a beach-themed production of the Charles Dickens holiday classic. Instead of a wintry-England-Cratchit working his cold fingers to the bone, beach-dwelling-Cratchit toiled into the wee hours making surfboards at the beach supply factory, pushed on by the relentless Scrooge.

Jack chuckled.

It might sound corny, but it was sure to be fun. Especially with musical numbers and a finale by Carol Reston, the Grammy Award-winning singer who resided in Summer Beach. He'd heard that Carol and her husband Hal had made a generous donation for supplies and marketing to kick off the inaugural season of the Seashell, the new amphitheater. Similar to the Hollywood Bowl in

Los Angeles, though smaller in size, the venue was sure to bring in visitors to help support the local community.

Jack understood this first production needed to be a success. For him, this wasn't only a pleasant diversion but also a way to give back to the community that had welcomed him. He'd never thought about leaving New York, but then, he'd had a lot of surprises lately.

A son. A dog. A beach cottage. A different career.

And Marina.

As he thought of her, he felt her presence and glanced behind him. Sure enough, she walked in, noticed him, and took a seat on the other side.

Jack's chest tightened; he deserved that slight. Worse, Cole was with her.

Leo tugged his sleeve. "Dad, Marina is here. Can we sit with her?"

"Not now. You can talk to her later." Jack motioned to Kai and Axe. "The reading is about to begin, so we have to pay attention. This is like school, only better."

Eagerly, Leo faced the front.

Jack was painfully aware that he'd been remiss in asking Marina out. He'd told her he was busy, but that had been the easy explanation. The truth was more complicated.

His record with women wasn't great. Not that he was a complete jerk, but there had been a time when he'd never known if he would live through the day. Threats, retaliations, bomb scares—he'd been investigating some nasty characters, and they played hardball.

Just when he'd plan to wind down, there had always been another story to pursue. He'd pack a bag, wish his girlfriend well, and take off to spare her worse heartache. The thought of being married and possibly leaving behind a wife and children scared him. The alternative was to take the safe assignments as many of his married colleagues did. Soon, they were off the road, and their plum assignments came to him. The story that brought him the Pulitzer had been one of those.

Admittedly, Jack was having trouble downshifting into life in the slow lane. While he'd welcomed the change, sometimes he was restless, but he couldn't leave Leo. And he feared he'd take out his frustration on Marina, which would negate any chance he had with her. He'd been an idiot to think he could string her along. A beautiful, accomplished woman like that—it was no surprise that a guy like Cole had come along.

With his gut churning at the thought, he bit his lip. What could he do about it?

Suddenly, Leo nudged him. "Dad, pay attention."

"Jack, are you with us?" Kai was talking to him. "Cratchit is up. Go ahead."

Quickly, Jack flipped the page and began to read. "At the factory, Surfboards by Scrooge, Bob Cratchit, wearing a tattered T-shirt and hoodie, is sanding surfboards by a dim light while Scrooge refuses to provide more light or better tools."

Adopting Cratchit's meek demeanor, Jack read the line. "Maybe next year we could afford new sandpaper, sir." He held up his hand as if clutching a shred of gritty paper.

"Use the edges," Axe bellowed. "You're being wasteful again. Look at all these scraps in the trashcan." He pantomimed flinging bits of sandpaper from the rubbish.

People chuckled, and Jack continued reading.

Presently, the action shifted to Scrooge's nephew Fred, played by Mitch Kline, the proprietor of Java Beach.

Mitch shoved a hand through his spiky blond hair. "Fred enters: A genial surfer dude who loves Christmas. 'Hey, Uncle Scrooge. We're chillin' at the Christmas party again this year. Why don't you come hang with us?'"

Everyone laughed at Mitch's spot-on delivery and slang.

Perfect casting, Jack thought smiling. He liked Mitch and recognized the younger man's keen entrepreneurial skills, though his manner was relaxed and easy going.

They continued reading through the scenes, with Kai and Axe performing brief lines from the musical numbers.

Kai tapped her script. "This is the family dinner at the Cratchit's scene. Leo is Tiny Tim." She glanced around the room. "Raise your hand if you're one of our young extras."

Leo beamed, and his friends Samantha and Logan shot up their hands.

Brooke's three sons also waved their hands.

"You're the Cratchit children, and you'll be gathered around a table," Kai said, holding hands out to the children, who joined her in the front. "When the audience meets Tiny Tim, they'll see he is quite sick. He might be confined to a bed, but he's the happiest of them all."

"I know how to do that," Leo said, sharing a look with his father.

Jack knew he was thinking about his mother, and how Vanessa had always been optimistic, even when she had been suffering with her illness.

Kai touched his shoulder. "That's good, Leo. Now, let's hear you read your part."

As Jack listened to his son read with the added voice inflection and gestures, pride swelled within him. Leo was a natural.

The rest of the script reading went well, and Jack was

happy for Kai and Axe that there were a lot of laughs at the right times. He saw them making notes on their scripts, so he figured they'd make a few changes as often happened at this stage, especially for a new script.

Throughout the reading, Jack tried not to stare at Marina, but he still found himself drawn to her. He understood that Cole was an old friend. Yet, Jack recognized the look that Cole had for Marina; it was a guy thing, and it was clear where Cole wanted this relationship to go.

Cole seemed like a decent man. Usually, Jack was happy for the women he'd left behind. He told himself they had done better without him in the end.

Not this time, however.

As fair as Jack was trying to be, that old mindset no longer served him well.

8

*M*arina tied one of Ginger's plaid flannel shirts around the waist of her blue jeans and started up the steps to Cole's motorcoach. The massive vehicle was emblazoned with flashy blue and silver streaks. It was a world apart from Jack's cozy, vintage Volkswagen van with its retro renovations. She thought about the time they'd taken it to the beach.

Feeling irritated at the memory, Marina pushed thoughts of Jack from her mind.

Cole was ahead of her, flicking on lights. He wore a suede vest over a flannel shirt and thick-soled boots. "Watch out. Those steps look a little steep for you."

"Is that a short joke?" Marina said, teasing him. She didn't mind her petite frame, even if she did carry a little more weight on it now, but she liked to see Cole squirm. Years ago, they used to trade friendly barbs over card games with Stan and Babs.

"No, ma'am," Cole said, grinning. "But I'll think of some if you want."

"And you can cut out the *ma'am* with me. I'm not your mother."

"Old habits are tough to break. Once a Marine—"

"Always a Marine. I know, but it's just us, Cole."

He laughed and lifted her up the last step. "You're still light as a feather. Welcome to the camper."

When he put her down, she looked up into his warm brown eyes. She should have been attracted to him right then, but maybe that would come later, she told herself. The memories of Stan and Babs still surrounded them. Glancing away, she said, "Wow. This is a palace on wheels."

The luxury motorcoach was beautifully outfitted. Deep navy blue, pearlescent white, and shimmering silver tones threaded through the cabin, from the plush club chairs to the full-sized sofa and built-in furnishings.

Marina swung around. Along one side of the coach was the kitchen area with a cooktop, a built-in refrigerator, and fine wood cabinets. A large-screen television was mounted across from the sofa. "It sure has all the comforts of home."

Cole stashed the groceries he'd brought in the refrigerator. "This gem came loaded. It has four roof air-conditioning systems, heated floors, a marble shower, and a tankless water heater for unlimited hot water."

"This is major glam-camping," Marina said, thinking about how much Kai would like this. "Is there a place to tuck my cranberry relish and cornbread so it won't fly around as we drive? I've been trying out new recipes for my holiday menu."

"I'll find a spot," he said, taking the dishes from her.

"There's a bathroom on the other side of the kitchen," he said. "The bedroom is in the back. If you need it for anything," he quickly added. "The sides slide out, so it will be even roomier once we arrive and set up."

"It's impressive," she said, noting the pride and exhilaration in Cole's demeanor. He clearly loved getting away. She found herself wishing she could travel like this, but with the time she needed to devote to the cafe, she would seldom have the opportunity.

Cole eased into the driver's seat, which reminded her of an airplane cockpit. After depositing her handbag, she sat in the large passenger seat, which was as cushy as a recliner. The windows were tall and wide, giving them excellent visibility.

Cole started the engine. "Ready to get under way?"

"Let's go," she said cheerfully. "While we're in the mountains, I'd like to collect pine cones and fir branches for the holidays." She planned to make wreaths and garlands for the cottage and the cafe. "We can't take them from protected parklands because they're needed for forest regeneration, but if we see a land owner, we can ask if they can spare some."

"You can do that while I drop a line and catch supper—unless you want to fish, too."

"Wouldn't I need a fishing license for that?" she asked.

He patted her knee. "Guess you're on pine cone duty after all."

They wound southeast toward the mountains and the lake that Cole had mentioned earlier. Soon, sand and palm trees gave way to mountain roads and pine trees. Even the air smelled different up here—fresh and invigorating.

Cole became more animated as they drove. "I'll drop a fishing line when we get there, but if I don't catch anything,

I also brought steaks or fish we can grill. Don't want you to think you'll go hungry out in the wilderness."

Marina had also brought some of Brooke's fresh produce for the cookout. "This reminds me of the camping trips we all used to take. Remember those?"

"It was nothing like this," Cole said, chuckling. "I think we borrowed a pretty shabby camper—a real camper, that is. You and Stan won the coin toss and bedded down in that, and Babs and I took the tent. It was a heavy, military surplus tent, not like the sleek models you find at the big box stores today."

Marina smiled at the memory. "And in the middle of the night, you and Stan crept out and started yapping like coyotes. We thought we were surrounded, and we were scared to death—until we noticed you guys were missing." Marina laughed, enjoying the ease of conversation.

Cole didn't seem to mind talking about Babs as long as they were including Stan. The four of them had been close during those years in the military, although Marina had lost touch with Cole and Babs after Stan died. With twins to care for, she barely had time for anything.

Her grandmother had been the backbone of their family for many years. Even as she and Brooke and Kai had grown older, Ginger had usually been available to help or talk—except when she was busy teaching school or away on a consulting assignment.

"I should bring Ginger up here again sometime," Marina said, taking in the scenery. "When we were kids, she used to bring us here to see the fall foliage and pick apples."

"You have a lot of good memories with her," Cole said. "I remember what happened to your parents, and I always felt bad for you. And then Stan died when you were pregnant...I wondered how you managed."

"It was rough," Marina said quietly. Even all these years later, she still missed her parents and Stan, especially during the holidays. But she'd learned to think of them fondly and often felt their presence.

Cole pulled the motorcoach as close as he could to the lake, although they still had a short hike. When he saw another man fishing by the lake, Cole stopped. After asking about the fishing and getting permission to collect a few cones from the man's property for personal use, they continued.

As they walked, Cole looked for a place to fish. He paused by the water's edge. "This looks pretty good."

"Do you fish a lot?" Marina asked.

"As often as I can. I hired a good management company for my properties this past year, so now I have more freedom. After the holidays, I'll take off and drive across the country to see the kids. They'll be with Babs after Christmas."

"They won't be with her on Christmas Day?"

"Not this time. They're both in love, which means they will be with their boyfriends' families. I feel bad for Babs, but she has her new husband, and plenty of friends."

"As I'm sure you do." She detected a note of sadness in Cole's voice as he spoke about Babs, but she supposed that was normal after their divorce. "Driving back east sounds like a grand adventure for you."

Cole hesitated as though something had been weighing on his mind. "How long do you think you'll stay at your grandmother's house?"

"I haven't really thought about it. The Coral Cottage is home to me, and I just opened the cafe."

"But you can close it anytime you want. Or find someone else to run it."

Marina didn't see where he was going with this, but she didn't like the way he was minimizing her efforts with the cafe. "I'm just getting started, and I really enjoy it. Running a cafe is something I've dreamed about for years."

"Is that what you really want to do at your age?"

"I'm not that old." Marina didn't quite know to respond to his question. "Actually, I thought I would be at the top of my career in broadcasting, but here I am starting over. And you know what? I'm having a great time."

"Maybe it could be even better."

"I'm pretty happy with my life right now." Marina felt a strange sensation coursing between them. Wherever Cole was going with that line of questioning, she wasn't ready to venture there yet. "Let's get your gear. You don't want to miss out on the fish." She turned and started up the slope to the motorcoach, digging in her boots for traction.

"I can carry it," Cole said, catching up with her.

Marina quickened her steps. "While you're doing that, I'll collect pine cones and fir branches."

Cole looked slightly disappointed, but he quickly recovered. "Come join me after you get what you need."

"Sure will," Marina sang out as she tucked the bags and clippers she'd brought under her arm. With her heart pounding, she started off at a brisk clip, following an uphill path toward the tallest trees.

"And watch out for mountain lions," he called after her.

Dangerous wildcats or not, it was all she could do to keep from running away.

Once Marina had put some distance between them, she leaned against a tree to catch her breath. While she might not be in the best of shape, that wasn't the reason her heart was threatening to explode.

Cole was the kind of guy who looked great on paper, but he had to be in charge. She recalled that about him when they were younger. Stan had been a take-charge personality, too. Still, her husband had respected and listened to her opinion. Perhaps Cole had mellowed, or maybe he was just on his best behavior.

Or was she overreacting?

Because of her unfortunate history with Grady—and add Jack to that list, now—she was being doubly careful.

To ease her mind, Marina took her time walking among the towering trees, listening to birdsong and streams bubbling down the mountainsides. Beneath big-cone pine and Douglas fir branches swaying in the slight breeze, she stepped onto a thick carpet of needles and brush. In the distance, the autumn colors of ash trees glowed orange and gold in the sunlight while sounds of wildlife scurrying near her footsteps filled the muted silence.

As Marina collected pine cones and snipped branches, she thought about the holiday season ahead. What she wanted most was to have her entire family around her, problems and all. She was so proud of Kai for plunging in and taking charge of the holiday show. After Dmitri destroyed her position with the touring company, her sister could have drawn the drapes and hidden in her room. No one would have blamed her.

And for that, Marina would endure the agony of seeing Jack at auditions. Supporting Kai's dreams was the most important thing she could do for her sister, who had helped her launch the cafe and was still there to wait tables when Heather was busy with school. Ginger loved pitching in and cooking, too. The Coral Cafe was a family affair, and Marina couldn't imagine abandoning it to cruise the country with Cole.

Marina paused and lifted her face to the leafy canopy above, breathing in the evergreen-scented air. She had a lot to be thankful for this fall.

Maybe Cole wasn't Mr. Right, but then, who was? If her expectations were too high, she might never find a partner. On the other hand, she wouldn't force herself into a relationship because of loneliness, like a too-tight shoe that ached all day and left your feet cramped. She'd had enough of that stiletto-lifestyle at the television station with the dangerously hip Hal and Babe. That was a situation that looked good on the outside but proved painful on the inside.

Surely she'd learned something from that—besides wearing shoes that cramped her style.

Resolving to stand up to whatever Cole had in mind, she started back on the path to the lake, pausing to collect pine cones along the way. She'd stood on her own after Stan died. There was no reason she couldn't continue to do that.

Yet now, after Heather and Ethan were pursuing lives of their own, her life had taken on a different rhythm. Cole had a point; living at her grandmother's home with her sister might not be what she wanted in the long term. Perhaps Ginger deserved some modicum of privacy, even if she professed she didn't.

To Marina, a home of her own appealed to her, though she had a gnawing feeling that it might be lonely. Even so, that might be welcome after spending a day at the cafe with customers.

She glanced down the slope at Cole. One thing was certain; life was always changing, and often when she least expected it.

On the way back, she stopped to stash her fresh wreath materials in the motorcoach. By the time she returned to the lake, Cole had a fish on the line.

"Looks like supper," Marina said, picking her way toward him through the low brush.

"This one can go back," he said as he reeled in the small fish. Gently removing the hook, he cradled the fish in his hands, speaking softly to it as he released it in shallow water. "Don't want the little guy too traumatized," he said, seeming a little self-conscious at his actions.

"I think that's kind," Marina said, seeing a different side to Cole.

"I wasn't always that way." He shrugged. "I brought some other food we can grill. How about I start a fire?"

"Sounds good to me."

"We'll do that near the camper."

Marina hesitated, thinking about the critters she'd seen and heard in the forest. "As much as I'd love to sit by a crackling fire up here, I'd hate for it to get out of hand and destroy a swath of land that's home to the local wildlife."

Cole stood, brushing his hands on his jeans. "I take a lot of precautions to make sure there aren't any embers that could ignite later."

"I'm sure you do, but you have a handy stove inside. I'd feel better cooking on that."

Cole laughed. "You haven't changed much. You were always concerned about the creatures."

"Was I?"

"Do you remember the dog we rescued? A neighbor had gotten a shelter dog to guard his property, only he left the poor creature tied up and was usually gone. You tried to talk to the guy, but he wouldn't listen and kept abusing the pup. So you organized a plot to rescue the dog and find a new home for it."

Marina smiled. "I'd forgotten about that. I'm pretty sure that's considered dog-napping now. Today, I'd call the authorities." As she strode toward the looming vehicle, she paused to turn back to him. "But I'd still do it again if I had to."

"See? You haven't changed."

"Actually, I have," she said with confidence. "I'm not the naïve young woman Stan married. I've become my own woman out of necessity and choice."

"Of course you have," Cole said, stroking his chin. "Shame on me for treating you otherwise—if it seemed I did."

"I just want you to know that."

"I guess I've changed, too," he said. "Life outside of the military took some adjustments. You expect people to follow orders in the chain of command, but it's not like that on the outside."

Marina smiled thoughtfully. Maybe he had changed. "No, it isn't."

"Friends? Let's start over as two more experienced—and a little beaten down—people." Cole dipped his head and reached for her hand.

For a moment, she hesitated, then slipped her hand into his gentle grasp. He seemed to need a connection—and a little compassion. She'd give him another chance. They walked on together.

At an odd tapping sound, Marina inclined her head. "What's that noise?"

Cole paused to listen. "Woodpeckers. Not all migrate, especially those in Southern California. They're preparing their winter quarters by chiseling out their roosting cavities."

She nodded toward the gleaming motorcoach ahead. "So, are you roosting in that this winter?"

"For the most part. I'll park it in the campground near the beach. It's only a couple of hours back to Los Angeles to check on my property if I need to. I have to trust the manager because I will be gone much longer in the future. I'd like to crisscross the country and visit friends along the way. Some I haven't seen since Afghanistan."

"That would be good for you," Marina said. She let go of his hand to climb into the motorcoach.

Cole expanded the interior by activating the automatic slide-outs. Soon, Marina was grilling turkey burgers and vegetables on the cooktop while Cole set up a pair of folding Adirondack chairs outside facing the lake. She scooped cranberry relish onto the cornbread, topped it with the turkey burgers, and added sides of salad and grilled vegetables.

"Wow, that's different," Cole said as they sat down to eat outside.

Marina smiled, watching him take his first bite. "I like to experiment. How is it?"

"Delicious."

They ate in pleasant, companionable silence, listening to the sounds of the wilderness surrounding them. Marina had forgotten how much she enjoyed being outdoors in the serenity of nature. Being near the ocean was exhilarating, but this was a different, calming experience.

After Cole finished eating, he put his plate aside. "Marina, I have something I've been wanting to ask you."

Her senses bristled. "What is it, Cole?"

"After the holiday show wraps up and Christmas is behind us, would you consider a trip with me? You said the cafe will be slow in the winter…maybe Ginger and Brooke could run it. You could fly back from Florida or I could drop you off in the spring."

Marina sucked in a breath. "That's a long trip, Cole."

"Just think about it for now."

"Cole, I don't need to—"

"Please don't answer yet," he said, cutting her off. "I know you're being careful about who you spend your time with, but I want you to know what I can offer you. You wouldn't get that with Jack."

"Excuse me? What does Jack have to do with this?"

Cole looked sheepish. "I stopped for coffee in the village yesterday. Some older guy was taking bets on who you'd end up with—Jack or me, seeing as how we're all in the holiday show. So, it sounds like you have a history with Jack."

"It's a short history," Marina said, clenching her jaw. Her chest tightened at the thought of Jack. "Was that Java Beach?"

"How'd you know?"

"It's Gossip Central. Be careful about what you hear there. Jack and I are finished." Marina rose and carried the plates inside before her emotions could overtake her better judgment.

9

*G*inger opened the door to the attic. "I have plenty of vintage beachwear that might be good for the holiday show." She flicked on the light at the top of the stairs.

Marina followed her grandmother into the attic. The musty smell reminded her of when she and her sisters would come up here to play. They loved to explore the old trunks that Ginger and Bertrand had carted across the globe.

Kai was right behind her. "That would be spectacular, Ginger. Poor Lizzy, having to return to Ohio to care for her mother during the holidays. She hadn't even had a chance to start on the costumes."

"She's a blessing to her mother," Ginger said. "As for the show, necessity encourages creativity. Now, open these trunks, and let's see what we can find."

Kai swung around, her jingle bell earrings chiming. "Where should we start?"

Ginger pointed to a dusty trunk in the corner. "That's

the one we carried from London to Paris," she said. "If we were performing the original Charles Dickens version of *A Christmas Carol*, we might find something in there. But for a beach holiday performance, I think not."

"I remember old necklaces and sarongs from your holidays in Hawaii," Marina said.

Ginger raised her brow. "Why, of course. Right over there." She pointed toward a trunk in a corner.

Marina lifted the lid of an old steamer trunk. Kai reached inside, and out came a flurry of Polynesian fabric in rich shades of coral and green.

"When I was a young bride, I made curtains from that fabric for this house," Ginger said with a smile. "They were quite divine. With these bright holiday colors, we could fashion sarongs or make flowing muumuus."

"Hmm, that could work," Kai said.

As Marina examined another length of fabric, she felt something rigid. Within the folds of the material was nestled a slim journal. She opened the cover. Inside were pages filled with letters and numbers—Ginger's ciphers and codes. Marina held up the journal. "This looks like yours."

A nostalgic look filled Ginger's face. "My first study guide. I was just learning then. That is an old trunk, indeed." She tucked the journal under her arm. "Is there anything else of interest in there?"

"Here's one of your dressy sundresses." Marina held up a red polka dot dress that was nipped at the waist with a full skirt. "This looks like it's from the 1950s or '60s."

"That was one of my favorite beach cocktail dresses." Ginger's eyes held a faraway look. "That was dubbed the New Look after the war. Christian Dior redesigned the slim silhouettes that fabric rationing necessitated, and Carmel

Snow, the editor of *Harper's Bazaar*, made it all the rage. When Bertrand was stationed in Paris, we once had a delightful evening with them. I don't know if I've ever told you about that."

"No. But I'm sure you will soon." Kai's eyes brightened. "We could add a short, red or cream cape over the shoulders, and this dress would be perfect for the part of Emily Cratchit. I think it would fit Leilani."

"It's so lovely," Marina said, running her hands over the shimmering taffeta fabric.

Ginger held the dress up to Marina. "With the right corresponding lipstick, that would be lovely on you, too, dear. You should wear red more often; it's such a happy color."

"We're looking for costumes, remember?" Kai took the dress. "One down, lots more to go. What about Bob Cratchit?"

Jack, Marina thought.

"Bertrand was about Jack's size." Ginger crossed the attic and unzipped a fabric-covered wardrobe. "I couldn't bear to part with some of his lovely clothes after he died. For practicality's sake, I donated most of them so that others could enjoy them as he did. But these pieces held special memories."

Kai put a finger to her chin in thought. "We'll put Jack in faded beachwear for the opening scenes, but I'd also like something nice that he would take pride in wearing with his family on Christmas."

"I know just the piece." Ginger drew a red dinner jacket from the wardrobe, gazing at it with reverence. "My dear Bertrand often wore this on Christmas Eve or Christmas Day with a fine, white voile shirt. He loved the festivities and always dressed the part. We were quite the smart pair. You should have seen us cut the rug."

Kai's eyebrows shot up. "Do what?"

"That meant dancing—we were fabulous on the ball-room floor." Ginger gave a dreamy sigh. "I'm so glad we made beautiful memories. I treasure them more than all the pearls he gave me."

Marina smiled. Ginger had shared those lovely strands with her granddaughters, so they each had something to remember Grandpa Bertrand by.

Kai added the red dinner jacket to her growing stack. "Jack will laugh when he sees this, but I can picture him in it. And with Leilani in the red polka dot dress, he'll be a perfect match."

"Just as we were," Ginger said on a wistful note. "Look at all the remnants of the life we led." Blinking back her emotions, she opened another box. "And here are baby clothes from Heather and Ethan. Maybe they'll want them someday."

"We can leave them here for now." Marina touched her grandmother's hand. While Ginger was sentimental, she rarely gave in to her emotions and preferred a more prag-matic approach to life. That had influenced Marina most of all, especially when she had the twins. Only through practi-cality and organization had she been able to manage two babies on her own. Even with Ginger's help, that had been a lot to handle. Her grandmother was still fully employed then, so most days, Marina had been by herself.

"Thanks for letting us mine your belongings for the show," Marina said.

Ginger brushed dust from her hands. "These things aren't doing anyone any good up here."

"We'll have everything cleaned and returned after the show," Kai said as she rummaged through trunks, plucking items they could use. "This will help us get a head start on the costumes. Since Axe is such a large man, his Scrooge costumes will probably have to be made to fit. But I'll check with costume shops in Hollywood first as we don't have much time."

"You'll manage to do it," Marina said. Throughout school, Kai had always figured out how to pull off projects at the last minute.

"It's not me I'm worried about," Kai said, chewing her lip. "Or Carol or Axe. It's the others who haven't acted before, or haven't in a long time, like Jack. Although he's such a professional, I'm not worried about him."

"It didn't look like the actors had too many lines to learn," Marina said, trying to steer clear of conversation about Jack.

Kai nodded as she looped clothing over her arm. "I wrote it that way so that much of the action and story is conveyed through the musical numbers. That way, our professionals are carrying the big scenes, with less seasoned actors providing the visuals. They have families and jobs, and for many, this is their first performance."

"It will be wonderful," Ginger said. "Since I'm narrating, I can cover for mistakes they might make."

"I appreciate that," Kai said. "We'll keep practicing in the ballroom at the Seabreeze Inn until the new stage is ready."

"I expect it will all magically coalesce on opening night," Ginger said.

"With a lot of hard work." Kai's eyes gleamed with excitement. "Still, I could use a little magic fairy dust. And I hope news of this reaches Dmitri so he can see what he missed." She spread her hand in an arc before her. "Kai Moore gets rave reviews in her directorial debut."

"Don't forget playwright," Marina added, grinning. "But do you really care anymore? Axe seems to hang onto your every word."

Kai pressed a hand to her heart. "He's such a sweetheart. A big old Montana teddy bear with one of the most beautiful voices I've ever heard. I don't know how I got so lucky, especially after Dmitri, the ultimate fake." She curled her lip in disgust at her ex-fiancé's name.

"Anything we should know about you and Axe?" Ginger asked.

"Oh, no," Kai replied. "I don't want to complicate our first show. This time, my job is at stake. And I've never had such a great opportunity."

"Wise decision," Ginger said, casting a look at Marina.

But Marina knew her sister. Kai never did anything halfway. She went for everything she wanted with passion, sang her heart out for every performance, and was crushed when things didn't go her way. Still, Marina had to admire the way Kai had bounced back after Dmitri. Maybe she'd learned something.

Ginger lifted a hand-painted music box from a carton and handed it to Marina. "Before we leave, I'd like to take a few items downstairs. It's time for their rotation." She selected a long, hunter-green cape from a wardrobe and passed it to Kai. "This will prove useful, too."

Although Ginger was still strong and sure-footed, Marina had noticed she was taking more care than usual. One of her grandmother's closest friends had suffered a sudden fall, and Ginger seemed more aware of potentially hazardous conditions. The stairs to the attic were narrow and steep.

"Is there anything else I can carry for you?" Marina asked.

"I'd love to have that tea set downstairs in the dining room this year. That was a Christmas gift from the French ambassador years ago. What a lovely couple they were, and what fun we had. I should call them this season to wish them a *Joyeux Noël*. They shared with us the finest places in Paris—not always the most expensive, mind you. Often they were little neighborhood restaurants that tourists seldom discovered, but they used the freshest ingredients and served traditional French fare. Not unlike what Julia Child made famous later."

"That was long before the internet gave away all the secrets," Kai said. "I'll help, too, Ginger."

"I'm so lucky to have you girls. You're the best gifts my daughter ever gave me." Ginger put an arm around each of them and drew them close. "Having my three girls—and my great-grandchildren—for the holidays is the most wonderful gift I could ask for. Don't think you have to give me anything else." She laughed softly. "Some people say miracles come in groups of three. I only have to look at you girls to know that's true."

Marina and Kai exchanged smiles. This is what Ginger always said, but they still managed to find or make things that delighted her. Often, they planned outings or little trips to surprise her. One year, they took the train to the Grand Canyon. Ginger still talked about that. Of all the places in the world she had traveled, she had never visited the Grand Canyon.

"But we love to pamper you," Kai said.

Ginger held up a finger. "Being in the inaugural holiday show is another magnificent gift that I'm looking forward to it. That green cape will be perfect for the cooler evening performances, although it might be a little heavy for sunny matinees." Ginger paused. "Why, this performance might even become part of my legacy."

Pausing, Marina frowned at Ginger's comment. "What do you mean by that?"

With a wave of her hand and an enigmatic smile, Ginger said, "None of us knows the number of days we're gifted, do we? But we all want to know we mattered."

Ginger had a studied air of nonchalance about her that Marina recognized. Kai didn't seem to pick up on it, but she was busy thinking about the show.

While Marina didn't think anything was wrong with Ginger, her grandmother often stated that her years on the planet were growing. That was true for all of them, but Marina resolved to watch Ginger and make sure this was a memorable holiday for her.

She couldn't imagine ever losing Ginger. Yet, Kai had Ginger's *joie de vivre*, and Brooke had her love of nature and cooking. Marina supposed she'd inherited her practicality. Still, there was so much they needed to learn from Ginger. Her sage advice, most of all.

Marina held out her hand to Ginger. "Let me help you down the stairs."

"Don't be silly," Ginger said, lifting her chin. "I still manage to hike mountains. But you can go first if you're more comfortable."

Marina exchanged a smile with Kai. While they would both look out for their grandmother, they wouldn't coddle her. They'd let her be the fabulous Ginger Delavie she had always been.

"We must live for the moment and make new memories every day," Ginger said as she closed the door to her treasured memories. "This Christmas, most of all."

$\mathcal{M}$arina swung her Mini-Cooper into the dirt parking lot by the amphitheater and turned to Kai. "Looks like a lot of the cast and stagehands responded to Axe's all-call for help today."

"That's a relief," Kai said. "Opening night will come sooner than we all imagine."

The scrappy little car bounced over ruts in the dirt, yet Marina steered through them. "I thought Axe would have the parking lot paved by the time the show opens."

"He's trying to get that done," Kai said, frowning. "He traded favors with another contractor, and that guy has been busy with paying jobs. It was okay this summer, but after the rain, it got a bit sloshy. It wasn't too bad in Axe's truck, but I know he'll get it done."

"You're going to have a lot more people for the holiday shows."

"We sure hope so," Kai with a grimace.

Her sister didn't sound as confident now as she had with the cast. "Are you selling many tickets?" Marina asked.

"The box office could be a lot better," Kai admitted. "We need to get the locals out to support us."

Marina turned off the engine and drummed her fingers on the steering wheel. "Maybe we could pitch tickets at the farmers market with Brooke. That's how we launched the cafe."

"Hey, that could work." Kai brightened. "All it takes is a little magic fairy dust, right? I'll toss some glitter, say *abra-cadabra*, and people will flock to buy tickets."

Marina laughed at the image Kai suggested, but it could be done. Looking at the other cars in the parking area, she said, "Ready to hammer and paint with the rest of your crew?"

"Let's go."

Marina stepped out of her car, wearing her oldest jeans and work boots. They were building and painting sets, and Marina was eager to see the newly expanded stage. She pushed up the sleeves of her old college sweatshirt. Today wasn't about being fashionable. Fortunately, she wasn't trying to impress anyone—and that included both Cole and Jack.

Especially Jack.

As she thought about him, her shoulders tightened. The fact that Kai cast Jack for one of the most important parts still bothered her. He'd never mentioned that he wanted to try out for a part, and who knew he could sing? He'd come to the cafe every day with Leo, and he could have said something about his interest.

Granted, there had been a couple of times when he'd wanted to talk, but she'd been slammed with orders and customers. Okay, more than a couple of times. But she was always busy at the cafe. That's why couples went out, she thought, still irritated that he hadn't asked her out again. She pressed her lips together. That was still more evidence that they were never a couple but merely convenient.

Maybe that was a little old-fashioned, but like Ginger often said, one must have standards. Marina wished she'd enforced that with Grady.

"Are you okay?" Kai asked, peering at her as they reached into the back of the car.

"Sure," Marina said, tearing her thoughts from Jack. "Why do you ask?"

"You're giving those supplies an awfully dirty look. I'm not sure what they did to you, but it must have been bad."

Marina made a face at Kai. "The sun was in my eyes. Here, take a bag." She plopped a sack of extra supplies they'd picked up at Nailed It into Kai's arms.

Marina glanced at the newly constructed, pearly white covering that was curved like a shell. At sunset, rays burnished the dome with a kaleidoscope of colors ranging from russet golds to twilight blues. The effect added to the magic of the venue.

Masking her displeasure over Jack, Marina turned to her sister. "I have an idea for a promotional slogan. How about Sunset at the Seashell?"

"We can work with that," Kai said, looping a bag of paintbrushes over her forearm. As they started toward the new stage, she slid a sideways glance at Marina. "So, out with it."

"What do you mean?"

"I can always tell when something is bothering you. You go overboard trying not to act like it."

Marina didn't want to have this conversation before they walked onto the set. "What would I be upset about?"

"My first guess is Jack."

"Okay, let's do this." Marina stopped and turned to face Kai. "Why did you cast him? Of all the people you could have chosen, you had to cast my ex?"

"First, I didn't know his status had actually changed in that little black book in your head, and second, he was the best choice by far. Axe thought so, too. This is about the show, Marina—not you. We have to put the best talent on stage for the inaugural performance. And this is my directorial debut, so I need people I can count on."

"But, Jack? Really, of all people…" Although Marina complained, Kai had a point.

"It's only for the holidays. And it's not like we have a huge pool of talent to draw from here." Kai made a face. "Besides, why should you care? You have Cole to play with now. Let that other fish swim free. Plenty of women will thank you."

"You can stop right there," Marina shot back.

Arching an eyebrow, Kai said, "Such a strong reaction for someone you don't care about anymore."

Marina ignored that comment, though it stung. "People are waiting for us, and we're late."

Kai grinned and added sarcastically, "Okay, Mrs. Scrooge. I'm glad we cleared the air on that. All I ask is that you have a good time. A lot of people are working hard to make this fun for everyone in the village."

With a sigh, Marina started off. "I'll try not to let him bother me," she said over her shoulder. Was she being mean-spirited or sticking up for herself? Some days the line was so fine she didn't know.

Behind her, Kai laughed. "You'll change your tune soon enough."

As they neared the stage, Marina could see that Axe was in his element directing volunteers on set building. Drop cloths covered the stage floor, and set pieces were taking shape from plywood and other raw material. Above it all, Chuck Berry warbled "Run Rudolph Run," over the sound system. Kai began to sing along.

Marina couldn't help smiling.

"Surprise," Heather said, poking her head up from the other side of a set piece and brandishing a hammer. Her blue-gray eyes were alight with happiness.

"What are you doing here?" Marina asked, her mood instantly brightening. She hugged her daughter. "I thought you had a paper due."

"You know how stressed I get about projects and exams," Heather said, tucking a strand of dark blond hair behind an ear. "I worked ahead and finished my paper last night, and then Aunt Kai called me. I wish I could be in the show, but it's during finals, and I'd be a mess. I'll come see it as soon as I finish my last test."

"We can always use extras if you have free time," Kai said.

"I'll keep that in mind," Heather replied.

Marina remembered what it was like to be young and feeling the pressure of exam season. "I'm glad you could come today. Is your brother here?"

"Over there with Jack." She nodded downstage.

Marina stiffened, and she could feel Kai watching her. "Thanks, sweetie."

Making her way toward Ethan, Marina tried to keep her gaze from shifting to Jack. She resolved to act cordial and upbeat. Today was meant to be fun for the volunteers

—and it was a critical day for Kai and Axe. Work had to get done, and she wouldn't risk jeopardizing that.

When she approached, Ethan looked up. He was the more gregarious one of her twins.

"Hi, Mom. What do you think?" Ethan stepped aside, showing her their handiwork. "This is a backdrop for the surfboard factory. You'll be looking at it from a distance, so it doesn't have to be perfect. Then we'll lean real vintage surfboards against it. Pretty cool, right?"

"You've done a great job with that," she said, nodding in approval at the painting-in-progress of a distressed brick wall.

"It was Jack's idea," Ethan offered. "And that old desk over there will be Scrooge's in the office set."

Marina realized that Ethan didn't know about the problems she and Jack had. Her son was living in San Diego, and his goal was to turn pro in golf. He was working at one of the top golf clubs and perfecting his game every chance he had. Ethan and Jack had become friends, and there was no reason that should change.

"I worked on the concept with Axe," Jack said modestly.

"Looks like you work well on a large scale, too," Marina said, allowing him a small compliment. His illustrations for Ginger's books were captivating. "Creative in one area, creative in others," she added lightly.

"Like cooking," he said, catching her eye.

"I suppose so." This was about all the time she could manage with Jack. "I'm on decorating duty, so I'll see you later, Ethan. Kai has more supplies if there's anything you need."

"Jack brought a lot of stuff, too," Ethan said. "New brushes and tools."

Looking a little self-conscious, Jack quickly added, "It wasn't much, but I figured Kai and Axe can use whatever help I can give them."

"That was thoughtful of you," Marina said, and she really meant it.

"We could sure use another hand here," Jack said.

Marina wasn't going to fall for that. "If I see anyone without work, I'll send them over. See you guys later."

She knew what Jack meant, but she had to get away from him. Yet when she turned around, she ran right into Leo, who flung his arms around her. Scout panted beside him, barely waiting until he jumped to lick Marina's cheek.

"Hi, you two," she said, laughing as she rubbed her cheek.

"This is so much fun," Leo said. "Come see what I'm doing." He took her hand and tugged her toward stage left. "Me and the other kids are painting the table we're using for the Christmas dinner scene."

"That's a fine look," Marina said, admiring his handiwork.

She greeted Samantha and Logan—Jack's nephew— and some of the other kids from Summer Beach. Brooke's boys were there, too. They were all working on the table and chairs. Dark red paint splatters dotted their faces and clothing, but they were having a good time. Some were wrapping empty boxes as gifts, while others were filling a cupboard with dishes and painting a turkey made of paper mache.

Working alongside Cole, Ginger waved to her. "Oh, Marina, dear. Come join us."

Marina made her way toward them. "What are you working on?"

Ginger gestured to a door that rested on a pair of sawhorses. "This will be at the entry to Scrooge's flat. It's for the scene where the doorknocker turns into his deceased partner's face. Only Cole is going to cut a hole in it, and we'll have an extra made up to look like a ghost to bring that scene to life."

"How clever," Marina said, smiling.

Cole looked up from his work. "While I build the set pieces, you and Ginger can paint them." He draped his arm across her shoulder. "Shall I get a brush for you?"

"I'll grab one from Kai and join you," Marina replied.

Although she saw Cole's gesture as a simple expression between old friends, it could be construed as more. She patted his hand and glanced at Ginger, who seemed happy to be productive. Marina wondered if her grandmother's energy might fade. "This will be a long day. Would you find a stool or a chair for Ginger?"

Despite Ginger's protests, Cole touched the brim of the baseball cap he wore. "I'll find some for both of you."

After he left, Ginger said, "How kind of Cole. Having a man around does have its advantages."

"I can carry chairs on my own," Marina said. "Don't get any ideas."

"Oh, I'm not the one with ideas. That man can't stop talking about you."

"We're just old friends," Marina insisted.

As Marina made her way across the stage that reminded her of a scene in Santa's workshop, she could feel Jack's eyes on her. Not only that, she could swear the Java

Beach crowd was murmuring among themselves and casting glances her way.

She remembered the bet. *Jack vs. Cole.*

Let them talk, she decided. When she was delivering the morning news, she'd learned that no matter what she did, viewers had an opinion. Besides the news, people often had an opinion on her style and dress. To one viewer, Marina's new jacket might be too conservative, and to another, the scarf she wore with it would be too flashy. And then there the hair comments: Too short, too long, too frizzy on a humid day. She'd had to rise above the chatter to focus on doing the best work she could.

That's what she would do now. Marina resolved to have fun today. She pushed up her sleeves, lifted her chin, and greeted people with a smile.

Everyone was here to spread the joy of the season and build a stronger sense of community. Through Ginger, she'd long been connected to Summer Beach. But now it was her home, and she had to make her way here. If that meant befriending people who were placing bets on her heart, that's what she would do.

Summer Beach was a small town; people would always gossip. Still, those same people would be the first to lend a hand when needed. They formed an extended family and were bonded simply by virtue of living by the sea—with its pleasures and occasional threats from nature.

Marina nudged Kai. "Got a brush for me?"

As Kai pulled one from her shopping bag, she whispered, "So it is Team Jack or Team Cole today?"

Making a face, Marina replied, "It's Team Marina."

"I like that." Kai laughed. "You go, girl."

Axe approached them, his arms held wide. "There's no

business like show business," he sang out in his deep baritone.

Kai belted out the next line, and Axe twirled her around, both of them laughing.

"The sets are coming along well," Marina said, happy to see them enjoying themselves.

"And we're glad you're a part of it," Axe replied, touching his forehead as if to tip a Stetson to her. "Kai, have a look at the set pieces and tell me what you think."

"They all look super," Kai said. "You must have started at sunrise."

"Not long after," Axe said. "That Cole is a machine. He and Jack are in some sort of race. They've built most of the set pieces. At this rate, we'll finish in half the time."

Marina couldn't help but smile. Competition had its benefits.

For the remainder of the morning, Marina worked with Ginger, Cole, and the rest of their crew. She noticed that Jack and Cole kept glancing at the other's work and increasing their pace—so much so that she and Ginger couldn't keep up. They had to add more volunteers to finish the final Santa's sleigh set piece. While not in the original story, Kai had added it at the end for the children in the audience.

As they finished, Ginger nodded toward Jack and Cole, who were congratulating each other. "That friendly competition worked out well for the theater," Ginger said. "Can't hurt to work in your favor, too."

"I'm not a prize to be won," Marina said. "Although it's flattering, I don't know that I'll choose either one of them."

"Maybe neither," Ginger replied cheerfully. "Just relax and enjoy the attention, my dear. Someday, you'll miss it.

Unless you're fortunate enough to have someone like my Bertrand, who was gone far too soon. That's why I'm so thankful to have my girls nearby."

Marina hugged Ginger. "I don't know what I'd do without you."

"Someday, you'll have to learn," Ginger said. "And then you'll impart my wisdom to the next generation—Heather and Ethan, and Brooke's tribe of boys. They'll certainly need it."

"Ginger, is there something you're not telling me? You've been saying things like this lately."

As her grandmother cleaned her paintbrush, she merely shrugged. "That's reality. We all have a time to go. Speaking of that, I would like to review my final wishes with you soon."

"You're not—" Marina's throat closed against the words she couldn't get out.

"Heavens, no. I am practical, though."

Marina nodded and managed to say, "Let's wait until after the holidays."

Ginger looked disappointed. "As you wish. But you'll find everything in my safe. You know the combination."

Did she? It doesn't matter, Marina insisted to herself. Ginger wasn't going anywhere this holiday season.

11

*J*ack stretched in bed in his cottage near the beach. The brisk air seeped through the window he'd left open last night, and it felt good against his burning limbs.

As a man who made his living with a laptop and a sketchpad, every formerly complacent muscle in his arms and torso screamed in agony. Why had he allowed Cole to goad him into a competition yesterday? At least they'd finished the set pieces in record time, and he'd managed to do one more than Cole.

It was a small elf for the final scene, but that little rascal counted. And it made a difference to Leo, who was keeping score.

Leo had been proud of him. That was a warm feeling Jack had never known before. His son had complete faith in him, and he never wanted to disappoint him.

Jack swung his aching feet onto the floor and flinched. He was paying for his actions today. Carefully, he hobbled to the bathroom, feeling at least two-hundred years old. He opened the mirror cabinet and swallowed a few over-the-counter pain reliever tablets. Cupping his hands, he drank cold tap water and splashed his face.

At least he could manage sitting in his small, sunny office off the bedroom. He could sketch out a new illustration idea for Ginger's book today.

"Morning, Dad," Leo said, bouncing into the open bathroom. "I'm ready."

"Yeah? Ready for what?"

"The jog on the beach you promised."

Jack leaned on the sink. "Right. About that…"

"I'm wearing the new running shoes you got me. See?" Leo ran in place double-time. "Bet I can outrun Samantha in these."

Jack gave him a tired smile. "I'm kind of worn out after yesterday. How about next week?"

Leo's enthusiasm evaporated, and his face crumpled. "But Samantha and her dad are meeting us on the beach. We'll be late if we don't leave now."

"Sorry, I forgot," Jack said quickly. He owed Samantha's father a debt of gratitude for looking after Leo all those years—before Vanessa had called Jack to come into Leo's life. More than that, he didn't want to fail Leo.

"Give me a minute to pull on some clothes." Jack hobbled back to his room.

"Why are you walking so funny?" Leo asked.

"I'm old—older than you, that is. Sometimes people my age walk like this in the morning."

Leo made a face. "Looks uncomfortable."

Jack stretched and swung around, loosening his torso and legs. "I'll be okay in a couple of minutes."

Leo wrinkled his brow with skepticism. "I sure hope so."

"Go brush your teeth," Jack said, mussing his son's hair. "We'll be out the door in five minutes."

"Great," Leo said, breaking into a grin again.

Jack stretched an old sweatshirt over his T-shirt and pulled on pair of thick jogging pants. The mornings were growing colder now, although the sun still broke through the marine layer and warmed the afternoons for a few hours. Winter at the beach was drawing near.

When he lived in New York, he loved getting out of the city during the winter and walking the cold, windswept coastline of New England. Sometimes he encountered sleet, but the air was brisk and invigorating, and it calmed the hectic city pace in his mind.

"Almost finished, Leo?" Whistling for Scout, Jack set off toward the front door.

The lanky Labrador retriever bounded around a corner, sliding on the hardwood floors. Chuckling, Jack reached down and scratched Scout behind the ears. "Hey, boy. Want to go to the beach?"

Scout snapped to attention and sat. His tail slapped on the floor as he waited for Jack to clip on his leash. Jack liked to let the dog off his leash at the designated dog beach. Scout had far too many distractions on the main beach. The last thing Jack wanted to do today was tackle a wet, out-of-control, over-grown puppy.

Jack held the door, and Leo bounded ahead of him. Once they reached the beach, John waved at them, and Leo sprinted toward Samantha.

Despite his burning muscles, Jack managed to fall into an easy jog alongside John.

"How are you feeling this morning?" John asked.

"Not too bad." Jack hated to admit his weakness.

John grinned. "If I'd worked at your madman-pace yesterday, I'd be paying for it today."

Blowing out a breath, Jack cast a sheepish glance toward John. "Is it that obvious?"

"We can take it easy until you work out the kinks." John slowed his pace while the kids ran ahead. "We'll catch up with Sam and Leo in a few minutes. As long as we can see them, they're okay."

Scout tugged against his leash. "Slow down, boy," Jack panted. "Heel, or do something."

While he wasn't in the shape that John or Mayor Bennett were in, he was getting there. At least his cravings for cigarettes had diminished, although at the first whiff of smoke, he still had a Pavlovian response to manage.

Scout looked back at him as if to laugh, but the dog finally took pity on him and slowed beside him.

John laughed. "That'll teach you to go up against a Marine."

"I don't know what you're talking about."

"Then you're the only one in Summer Beach who doesn't. I heard the odds shifted in your favor yesterday. I might have put a couple of bucks on you, too. No pressure, though."

Jack shook his head. "What kind of place is this that people do that?"

"It's a small town, Jack. The kind of place I grew up, so I get it. It's good that we can still give the kids this sort of upbringing. My tech consultancy has actually grown since we moved here. Since I'm not wasting time taking meetings,

I have more productive time." He grinned. "Small town folks are going to talk, so get used to it."

"I'm a farm boy, myself," Jack panted. "Even so, I got used to the anonymity of New York. I had my neighborhood spots I went to, but if you wanted to drop out of sight for a while, it was easy to do. I traveled a lot then, too. Nothing to tie me down, but I sure like having Leo now."

"It was like that in Los Angeles, too," John said. "Are things working out with Leo?"

"Pretty well," Jack replied. "And he made friends quickly in the neighborhood."

"We're glad about that," John said. "Just between us, Denise and I were surprised that you stepped up to look after Leo. A lot of men wouldn't have." He hesitated. "Have you talked to Vanessa lately?"

"That new, experimental treatment is doing wonders for her. She's looking good."

"Yeah, about that…"

Alarmed, Jack slowed. "Has something happened?" He counted Vanessa as a close friend, besides being the mother of his son. He prayed her illness hadn't returned.

"Not the way you think," John said quickly. "But I thought you should be prepared about a new development."

Jack felt tension seep into his shoulders. He could count on John to be straight with him. "For what?"

"The research team in Europe is so impressed with Vanessa's results, they want her to speak about her experiences."

"That's a good idea."

"They've asked her to go to Zurich."

"I'm always happy to take care of Leo."

"Right away, Jack. Before the holidays and through the new year. She wants to take Leo to Switzerland with her."

Jack sighed. "Leo will be awfully disappointed about the holiday play."

"I know," John said, sounding uncomfortable. "But, here's the deal…they might be gone a very long time."

Something in John's voice led Jack to say, "Don't tell me she's staying there."

Averting his gaze, John seemed at a loss for words.

"You're kidding, right?" Jack waited for a reply, but John only shook his head. "She can't do that." Jack had trouble breathing at the thought of not seeing Leo every day.

"Think about what precious time Vanessa has left," John said. "Maybe she'll have a normal life span, but no one knows until more studies are done."

Jack felt guilty for his selfish thoughts. He'd probably have many more years with Leo than she would, although he hoped he was wrong. "Does she have to stay nearby for more treatment?"

John took a breath. "It's not that. Vanessa has been talking to one of the researchers, Dr. Noah Hess, who is quite a renowned physician and scientist. Several times a day, in fact. He's met her in Los Angles with her medical team, and we had dinner with Noah and Vanessa last time we drove her there." John hesitated. "I think she's in love, Jack. That's why she's planning to move."

"Oh, geez." Feeling cast out of the picture, Jack pushed a hand through his hair. "I'm glad to know Vanessa has found someone, but Leo and I just connected. We still have a long way to go." Bitterness and dismay welled up inside of him. "I changed everything in my life for Leo. And I was happy to do it."

"She realizes that, and she doesn't know how to tell you."

"Wow. I didn't see this coming." Jack felt like he'd been socked in the gut. "Can't she wait until after Christmas?"

"He wants her to meet his children. They're grown, but I understand he has asked them to fly in to meet Vanessa and Leo."

"Sounds serious. I didn't think Vanessa ever wanted to get married."

"That doesn't preclude a relationship," John said. "After what she's been through, we should be happy for her and let her go." He cleared his throat. "This is hard on Denise, too. They've been best friends for years. We moved here for her—don't get me wrong, I'm glad we did—but Denise is really going to miss her. And Samantha is will be heart-broken to lose Leo."

"Poor kids," Jack said, thinking about Leo. "They've really bonded through all this."

John shook his head. "You have no idea. They grew up together, so they're more like siblings."

Vanessa had a right to her life, but Jack couldn't imagine himself without Leo now. He blinked hard, processing the information. "When?"

"As soon as school is out for the holidays. Vanessa hasn't told Leo yet, but she plans to this week."

Jack faced the ocean, letting the brisk spray sting his cheeks. "Leo can still be in the play until then. Kai can arrange an understudy to step into his role. We need this time together, John."

"I'll mention it to Vanessa. But you should talk to her.

Let me know when, and Denise and I will take Leo with us so you can talk."

Jack bumped fists with John. "I appreciate that."

Ahead of them, Leo and Samantha had turned around and were racing back to them. When the pair reached them, Leo hurled himself into Jack's waiting arms.

Jack swung Leo around, hugging him tightly as he tried to imagine what he would do without his son.

But it didn't have to be that way. Immediately, Jack thought about what he could do in Zurich. He could follow Leo; he could find work in Zurich. Or maybe he could continue to work with Ginger over the internet.

Then, feeling torn, he thought about Marina. Instantly, the weight of lost opportunity settled heavily on his chest. He'd thought that he and Marina would have plenty of time ahead of them.

Jack set Leo down and folded him in his arms. "I love you, Leo."

His son turned a radiant face to him. "I love you, too, Dad." Then he and Samantha scampered off again.

Watching them go, Jack had one thought.

Life simply wasn't fair.

12

"*G*et your red-hot tickets right here for opening night at the Seashell, Summer Beach's new amphitheater." Standing in the aisle of the farmers market, Kai waved a pair of tickets. Her earrings were blinking ornaments, and she wore a glittery sweatshirt that read, *A Christmas Carol...At the Beach.*

Behind her, Marina laughed, thinking about how her sister had helped launch her muffins and brownies at the market after arriving in Summer Beach.

"Can't miss her, all dressed up like a Christmas tree," Brooke added as she arranged her organic winter vegetables on one side of the table and Marina's cranberry-orange muffins and pumpkin bread on the other side.

"Wait until she starts singing," Marina whispered.

"I heard that," Kai said. As if on cue, she began humming a show tune from *Auntie Mame* before bursting into a rousing rendition. "We need a little Christmas..."

Shoppers slowed to listen to Kai.

"Now," Marina whispered to Brooke. They began to pass out flyers.

Kai winked at her as she built to the crescendo. The crowd and fellow vendors burst into applause, and Kai executed a theatrical curtsy, smiling broadly. "Come to our inaugural holiday show. Tickets are available right now, but like Santa's milk and cookies, they're going fast."

"Speaking of that, free cookies with every ticket sale," Marina called out. "White chocolate and macadamia nut with cranberries, a seasonal favorite at the Coral Cafe. And while you're at it, be sure to reserve your holiday picnic boxes for the performance at the Seashell."

A young couple stepped up to the table. "Is the show suitable for children?" The woman asked.

"Absolutely," Kai said. "I wrote it with children in mind, and many of our local Summer Beach youth are performing in the production. We have a special guest appearance at the end of every show, too." Kai put her hand to her mouth as if sharing a secret. "He'll be wearing a red suit, and his initials are S.C."

"That sounds like fun," the woman said to her husband. "What dates do you have tickets available for?"

"Marina can answer that," Kai said merrily.

"I'd be happy to," Marina said. "Would you like opening night? I think we have a few good seats left." She pulled out a calendar.

After the couple decided on the date, they inquired about the picnic boxes.

Marina gestured to a photo she'd taken of their holiday picnic box. She had created variations for vegetarian, gluten-free, and diabetic diets.

"In our most popular box, you'll get roasted turkey and

cranberry relish sandwiches with homemade sweet potato chips, our organic chilled broccoli salad, and pumpkin bread—with or without rum-soaked raisins." She pointed out the variations and handed them a printed menu.

"Let's order," the husband said. "Sounds delicious and probably better than we could assemble."

"Great. My sister Brooke will add that up for you." Marina scooped up several cookies she'd baked and slid them onto napkins. "Thank you, and enjoy the show."

Marina turned to Kai and clapped. "Encore, encore."

Kai inclined her head. "With pleasure."

As she regaled the gathering crowd with "It's Beginning To Look A Lot Like Christmas," Marina and Brooke sold tickets and reserved holiday picnic boxes.

Soon, a large crowd gathered in the farmers market, and Marina spotted Jack and Leo standing at the edge. Leo watched Kai in awe and wormed his way through the crowd with Jack and Scout in tow. Leo was such an adorable child, and he was so happy acting on stage as Tiny Tim. She wiggled a finger at him, beckoning him over.

"Are you getting excited?" Marina put a cookie in a napkin and slipped it to him.

Leo nodded enthusiastically. "This is the best thing that's ever happened to me. Except for getting a new dad."

Jack slid his arm around Leo's shoulder and knelt beside him. "You'll be great, buddy. This is a show we'll never forget."

Something about the way he pressed his cheek against Leo's stirred Marina's heart. Yet, Jack wore a strange, sad expression. When Leo turned to watch Kai, Jack stood with his hand on Leo's shoulder, watching his son instead of the performer.

It was hard to believe this was the same man she'd seen at the theater trying to outdo Cole on building sets. Something had recently transpired to transform Jack. Marina wondered if Vanessa had taken a turn for the worse. Perhaps he was bracing himself to care for Leo.

Before Marina knew what she was doing, she reached out to him, whispering, "Jack, is everything okay?"

Jack took her hand and looked up into her eyes as if he were seeing her for the first time. His gaze held such a mixture of love, recognition, and regret that she was taken aback by its intensity.

"I've made a lot of mistakes," he began in a husky, emotionally-laden voice. "But I've never wavered in how much I care for you."

"Jack, you don't need to explain."

"No, I do," he said, still holding her hand. "May I take you out on your night off?"

Though Marina tried to keep her composure, her heart tightened at his words. "I think we both know it's too late for that."

"Then a walk on the beach," he said quickly. "Like we used to. I need to talk to you about something." His face flushed. "I don't mean to come between you and Cole. It won't take long."

Marina had to diffuse the intensity of this confusing situation. Averting her gaze, she slipped her hand away. "I'm sorry, but I'm really busy."

"Just a few minutes. Please?"

She had never heard Jack plead with her, and it was unsettling. He seemed so vulnerable. Brooke caught her eye and gave her a slight nod.

Marina couldn't believe she was doing this, but she

turned to Jack. "I can meet you this afternoon." She named a time.

Relief flooded his face. "How about by that big rock near the Coral Cottage? Do you know the one?"

"I'll see you there." Marina and her sisters had played a game called Queen of the Sea, and they'd raced each other to scramble to the top of the rock. They'd made up a story about how it had been dredged from the sea by a mermaid queen to watch over the beach.

Kai finished her song, and applause filled the air. She held her hands to Leo. "And here is one of the stars of our show, Leo Ventana. Let's hear it for our young star. Leo, take a bow."

Leo looked like he would burst with excitement, and he bowed toward the crowd several times. "I hope you'll come to the show," Leo said, waving. "This will be so much fun. For you, too."

Everyone laughed, and Leo was clearly enjoying sharing the limelight with Kai. But Marina's attention was on Jack. His eyes held a bittersweet gaze, and he ran a hand across Leo's shoulders as if he might lose him at any moment.

Brooke leaned toward her. "What's bothering Jack?"

Marina watched him. "I have no idea, but he's changed."

"Maybe Jack is going to concede defeat to Cole."

"Don't tell me you placed a bet, too."

Brooke shook her head. "My money is always on you."

"Cole is just a good friend." Marina was saddened by these thoughts, but she realized Brooke might be right. She would meet with Jack.

"You're the only one who believes that," Brooke said,

arching a brow. "Cole's a good guy. A lot of women are watching what's happening between you two."

"Really, Brooke. It's not like that."

"I see the way he looks at you."

"Get your tickets for the show right here," Kai said, swinging around to motion to Marina and Brooke. Marina quickly shifted her thoughts, though she watched Jack and Leo walk away with Scout trotting beside them. Even the dog seemed subdued.

When the market ended, Brooke tallied their receipts. They had sold out of her vegetables and Marina's baked goods. Ticket sales and picnic box reservations were impressive, too.

"We had a great day," Brooke said.

"Thanks to Kai's magic fairy dust," Marina said. She wrapped her last two cookies in a napkin. "I'm going to take these to Cookie O'Toole. I'll be right back."

As Marina cut through the thinning crowd, she saw Cole standing to one side with a phone. She wanted to talk to him, but she hated to eavesdrop. She waited nearby.

"It's good to talk to you, too, Babs," Cole said.

Hearing this, her ears pricked up. She had spoken to Babs yesterday, and they'd had fun catching up and laughing over their antics in the past. Marina had said that Cole was passing through Summer Beach, but she didn't want to give her the impression there was anything more than friendship between them. Yet, Marina's respect for him was growing. Even though Jack had narrowly beaten him in set building, he'd been gracious about it.

Still, she missed Jack's keen wit and intelligence. It would be good to talk to him, she thought, deciding that Brooke might be right.

She didn't like the idea of being the prize, but Ginger would tell her she should be proud of that. Her grandmother's words floated back to her. *Someday, people won't look at you as they once did.* Marina had bristled against that because she had worked hard all her life to be judged not on her looks but on her abilities.

As she waited, she couldn't hear Cole's exact words, but she could tell from his voice that he was enjoying the conversation. She'd thought Babs had devastated him. Yet, perhaps Babs had paid for that in the end. Marina couldn't be sure, but when she asked Babs about her new husband, she'd changed the subject. Not once, but twice.

Even though it had been years since Marina had seen her friend, she had known her well. She had a sense that Babs wasn't happy in her new marriage. Perhaps she regretted it.

Cole tapped his phone, pocketed it, and turned around. "Marina, I didn't see you there," he said, looking surprised.

"Just passing by," she said.

"That was Babs," Cole said, looking down at his phone. "She said the two of you spoke, and she wanted me to know."

"We were good friends, and I simply wanted to catch up."

Cole seemed embarrassed—as if he'd been caught at something. "It could be awkward, that's all."

"We were all good friends, Cole. Nothing has changed, except that Stan is gone."

Yet as Marina spoke, she realized that in Cole's mind, something had changed. However, she wasn't sure what.

13

"*D*eck the halls with boughs of holly…" Kai's voice greeted Marina as she walked into the Coral Cottage. On the door was taped a piece of paper in Kai's handwriting that read, *Costume Fittings Here. Come In!*

"Hi, everyone," Marina said as she shrugged out of her navy blue anorak and hung it on a coat stand by the door. She had worn a lightweight, navy-and-white striped sweater under her chef's jacket for the lunch run. Here at the cottage, the sun was bright, a chill was in the air, and the holidays were in full swing as preparations for opening night continued.

"How was lunch at the cafe?" Kai asked.

"Fairly steady. Heather did a great job filling in for you, but customers missed you."

"They're going to love the show, though," Kai said. "Where are my actors?" she called out.

As Axe and Jack entered the room in their show outfits, Kai motioned to them. "Please turn so I can see the clothes from all angles."

Sitting on the sofa, Leo and Samantha watched with round-eyed excitement.

Last night, Marina had helped Kai arrange changing areas for the women in Kai's bedroom and the men in Ginger's study. Her sister would be busy all day.

"Smells yummy in here," Marina said, watching Jack. The fragrant aroma of hot apple cider wafted from the kitchen. She'd added her grandmother's cider recipe to the menu, along with her own cranberry-orange muffins. Customers loved the seasonal favorites on the Coral Cafe menu.

"Ginger is in the kitchen," Kai said. "We're in full holiday mode here."

In the center of the living room, Kai snapped photos of Jack and Axe in costume. As artistic director and Jill-of-all-trades, she looked her part today, clad in a black sweater and black leggings with her thick strawberry blond hair hastily clasped in a ponytail. Kai paused to consider the two men as they turned slowly in front of her.

Jack was costumed as poor over-worked Bob Cratchit in a tattered hoodie and worn trainers—his own, Marina knew. Axe appeared as tightwad Ebenezer Scrooge in a drab brown coat and dingy khakis.

"Bah humbug," Axe bellowed, jabbing his fists to his hips with a scowl.

Kai laughed. "I think you've got that down. But Jack, you'll need a more haggard expression to go with that costume. As for you, Axe, I think we can do better than that jacket. I'll sketch a couple of ideas later so you can see the direction I'd like."

Marina could feel Jack's eyes on her. Yesterday, when a vendor arrived that she needed to talk to, she'd had to put off the walk Jack wanted. Then, he had to pick up Leo from school, so they'd postponed it. She couldn't imagine what was so important that he wanted to discuss, but she assumed it had something to do with Leo. She and Jack were finished, after all.

At the door to the kitchen, Ginger appeared. She wore an apron embroidered with the words, *From the Kitchen of Mrs. Claus*, over her cream-colored corduroys and a red cashmere sweater. "Would you like some hot apple cider?"

"That sounds delicious." Marina rubbed her hands together. In the winter, the sun warmed the beach for only a few hours in the afternoon. The old cottage could be a little drafty. "Shall I start a fire to knock off the chill?" She needed to do something to keep busy around Jack.

"Sure," Kai said. "It's getting a little nippy in here."

Marina knelt before the hearth, added twigs they'd collected from the yard, and stacked logs in the fireplace. After lighting and coaxing flames, she turned around and caught Jack watching her.

Just then, Leilani appeared in the hallway behind Jack. She wore the red polka dot dress that Ginger had stored in the attic.

"Wow, you look amazing, Leilani," Marina said, quickly shifting her gaze from Jack. Although she was being perfectly cordial and treating him as she would anyone else here, she could feel the tension between them.

Or was it her imagination? She fanned her face. "That fire is going to warm us up quickly."

Kai clicked her pen and made a few notes in a moleskin notebook. "Jack, I'd like to see you in the red jacket next. I want to look at it with Leilani—Mrs. Cratchit—to see how you two will look together for Christmas Eve dinner at Chez Cratchit."

"Can I help you with anything?" Marina asked. She was impressed with Kai's organized approach. Her sister was more of a free spirit, and Marina had only seen her professional work in on-stage performances. This managerial role was new for Kai, and Marina was glad to see how seriously she was taking it. Kai was blossoming.

Her sister looked relieved at the offer. "Would you take photos of the outfits? That will save time. I need to make sure alterations are just right." Kai motioned to the woman who stood next to Leilani. "Would you two come here while Jack changes?"

"This is so exciting, and I just love this dress," Leilani said, twirling to the center of the room. She held out the full skirt of her red-and-white polka dot dress.

"You're going to look fabulous in this on stage," Kai said. She pinched the shoulders of the dress and turned to the wardrobe supervisor, Louise, who also ran the Laundry Basket dry cleaners in the village. "Ginger is taller, and the shoulders poke up a little high. Do you think we can alter the shoulders to fit Leilani better?"

Louise nodded, her steel-gray hair flashing in the winter sun that shone through the cottage windows. "That's easy enough. It fits well in the bodice, though, and the length is good." Taking steel pins from a small red cushion that she wore strapped to her wrist, she pinned it to fit. "How is that?"

Kai eyed the dress. "Turn, please, Leilani."

As Leilani did, Samantha watched, wide-eyed. "That's so, so pretty. I wish I could have a dress like that."

Denise spoke up from her spot on the sofa. "Do you think you can make that dress for my daughter?"

"I'd be happy to," Louise said. "I have her measurements, so I can make a pattern for her from this dress. That would be cute for the holidays, especially with a little faux fur white wrap. I could make that, too."

"That sounds adorable," Denise said. "We're going to have some special events this year."

"Thanks, Mom." Samantha beamed with excitement while Louise made markings on Leilani's dress with white tailor's chalk.

"How about a capelet over this dress?" Louise asked Kai. "It will be pretty chilly at night during the performance."

"I'd appreciate that," Leilani said, shivering a little.

Kai considered it. "I prefer the look without a cape, but since we're not in a heated theater, I suppose we should. I don't want the cast coming down with pneumonia. I've seen that happen."

"A thin wool capelet would drape well with the dress and not add too much bulk," Louise said. "I think I have one that I can donate to the cause."

"It's not too fancy, is it?" Kai asked. "The Cratchits aren't wealthy."

"It should be fine," Louise said.

Moments later, Jack reappeared with dark slacks, a white voile shirt, and their grandfather's cranberry-red dinner jacket.

Marina drew in a breath at the sight of him. The jacket fit him in all the right places.

"Bravo," Ginger said as she delivered a cup of hot cider to Marina. "Bertrand would be proud of you in that. I suspected you were about the same size. I've always liked broad-shouldered men."

Warming her hands on the mug, Marina smiled at Ginger's comment, although she had to admit he looked nice.

As if Kai read her mind, she said, "Maybe too nice for Cratchit."

Jack stroked the sleeve. "Wouldn't my character save one good jacket for holidays?"

"How about a slightly tattered knitted scarf?" Marina suggested. "It's not especially beachy, but would that matter for the holiday scene? And Leilani will look smashing."

Meeting her gaze, Jack smiled slowly. "That would work, wouldn't it, Kai?"

"I think it would. In green, I should think. Or black. We'll see what we can find. Brilliant, Marina." Kai made notes in her book. "We should change the pants and the voile shirt to something more casual."

"I have a couple pants that could work," Jack said.

"Bring them to rehearsal." Kai turned to Marina. "Would you take photos of Jack? From all sides, please."

Feeling self-conscious, Marina snapped photos as Jack turned. A lazy half-smile curved Jack's lips, not that it mattered. "There, that's it," Marina said, perhaps a touch too brightly. "Next?"

"Jack, stand by Leilani now," Kai said, easing onto a stool and adjusting her scarf. "I want to see you two together. Act naturally."

"Right." Marina shot a few more photos.

Kai looked up at Ginger. "Let's see how that cape you brought down works on you."

While they waited for Ginger, Kai looked at outfits for Leo. She'd shopped thrift stores for his outfits and others. "Let's see the flannel pajamas for your bed scene first, and then the faded jeans and a bulky cream sweater for the holiday feast."

"Oh, boy," Leo said, dashing into the men's changing area.

Marina laughed. "We should all be as enthusiastic as Leo."

"He's so happy acting the show," Denise said. "I know Vanessa will love seeing him on stage, even for a few shows."

"Excuse me?" Kai turned toward her.

"I meant for the few shows for this holiday season," Denise said. Color rose in her cheeks. "Someone else could do it next year."

Kai inclined her head. "With his love for theater, I think Leo is just getting started. He's a natural. Maybe Vanessa doesn't realize that."

"She's in for a real surprise," Denise said. "Samantha loves this, too."

As Marina listened to the exchange, something about it struck her as odd—not what Denise said, but how she sounded. As if she'd let information slip that she hadn't intended.

Or maybe she was just reading more into it. When Leo emerged, Marina snapped photos, and he acted like it was a real photoshoot. She laughed. He was a natural. Maybe he got that from his father.

After they'd finished with Leo, Ginger made her entrance. She wore a floral muumuu in cheery red flowers and palm fronds that Marina recalled from photos. She topped it with the hunter-green cape she'd found upstairs. Ginger swished regally into the room and struck a pose.

"How is this for Madam Narrator?" Ginger's rich stage voice carried through the room. "I can have a hat made to match—perhaps festooned with seashells and starfish. I'll perch on a stool and guide our gentle attendees through the performance."

Kai chuckled. "It's perfect, Ginger. You might steal the show."

"I have every intention of doing that—in my way," Ginger said. "We'll all conspire to make this a smashing success."

Kai and Louise continued to work on each outfit for characters and scenes as cast members arrived, took their turns, and left. For Carol Reston, Kai had arranged a private wardrobe consultation at her home, saying that Carol was going to mine her closets.

Marina wondered what Carol's Ghost of Christmas Present would look like. She could hardly wait to see the costume in the dress rehearsal. Whatever it was, she was sure it would be fabulous.

After everyone was gone, Kai flopped onto the sofa. "That was intense. But isn't it going to be magical? I love it when the costumes start to take shape."

"What do you want me to wear?" Marina asked, nudging her. "I'm only an extra, but maybe I have some-thing in my closet. Or I can raid Ginger's trunks again."

"Oh, my gosh, I can't believe I forgot about you," Kai said, slapping her forehead. "Every extra is important, but especially you. We probably have a lot of beachwear in our closets. I've been telling people to layer thin silks or long-johns under them for added warmth."

Marina dropped onto the sofa next to her and laughed. "Don't worry about it. We'll find some things." She flung an arm around her sister. "What you're doing is pretty gutsy and impressive. Have I told you I think you're amazing?"

Kai leaned her head on Marina's shoulder. "That means a lot for me to hear you say that. I know I was only a kid when our parents passed away, but at times like this, I often wonder what they would have thought."

"They would have been so proud of you," Marina said softly, stroking Kai's wavy hair. "Losing them was tough on all of us, but Brooke and I had more time with them, so we have more memories to comfort us. I've often thought that you had it hardest, because you were so young. You had a gaping hole in your life with little to draw on to ease your grief."

With her eyes welling with emotion, Kai looked up at Marina and took her hand. "I had you and Brooke and Ginger, and you all doted on me. I've always counted my lucky stars for that."

Blinking back tears of her own, Marina pressed a hand to her heart. "They're always with us, and I know they're smiling down on you and giving you a high-five as they always did."

"I remember that," Kai said, smiling. "Not much else, but I have a clear picture in my mind of that."

Marina hugged her close. "I have the best sisters in the world."

"That's funny—so do I." Marina wiped the corners of her eyes.

Ginger returned to the living room, having returned the cape to Louise for the costume wardrobe. "What are all these tears? This should be a happy, momentous occasion."

"We were just talking about Mom and Dad," Marina said. "And about how proud they would be of Kai."

"Oh, yes, indeed." Ginger wrapped her arms around both of them. "I often feel their presence, but particularly during the holiday season. How they loved to plan a special Christmastime for all of you. They would love this show, and I'm sure they would have insisted on being in it, too."

"I'm so thankful for such a wonderful cast," Kai said. "Especially Leo. He's going to steal the show—even from you, Ginger."

"Those young rascals always do," Ginger said with a theatrical huff. "He'll make a wonderful Tiny Tim."

Marina frowned, recalling what Denise had said. More than that, it was her demeanor that was disturbing. She glanced at Kai, wondering if she should share her suspicions with her. Yet, Denise's comment hadn't seemed to faze her, so Marina let it go.

Kai was in charge here, and it wasn't Marina's place to interfere. If there was a problem, Kai would handle it better than she could anyway.

14

*K*ai clapped her hands. "Places everyone. We'll run through the entire show from the top—no stopping this in the final dress rehearsal. And be careful with your costumes. Imagine that this is opening night, and you're going to be fabulous—the best you've ever been. Tonight will be the same as opening night, except the big man in the red suit will be paying us a visit then."

Everyone was excited over the costumes and sets that would help them create the holiday magic. As a cheer among the cast and crew went up, Marina wondered who Kai had found to play the role of Santa Claus. She'd kept that a secret.

Over the past few days, Marina had helped Kai and Axe with rehearsals at the new venue. She'd brought salads and sandwiches—and kept New England clam chowder and shrimp bisque simmering on hot burners backstage.

Kai and Axe had also coordinated with Celia's school music program. Now, the small orchestra pit was filled with young musicians, as well as a few local residents Axe had coaxed from retirement. Dressed in dark clothing, they were tuning their instruments and eagerly awaiting their cues.

Spirits were high, and Marina loved being backstage with the cast and crew. This was a true Summer Beach effort, and everyone expected the new Seashell theater would bring more visitors to the village. Marina was ready for her part as a beach caroler extra in the first scene. She wore a flowing beach caftan with warm winter silks she'd used for skiing underneath.

These last few days, Brooke had been happy to step into the kitchen at the Coral Cafe and cover for Marina. During the show, the part-timers she had trained would handle the last shift, but as the holidays drew nearer and the evenings grew cooler, her business had significantly declined in the evening. People were busy shopping and planning trips.

Brooke had also overseen the picnic box preorders. Chip would manage distribution at the venue while Brooke joined the cast as an extra alongside Marina. They were all there to support Kai.

As cast members hurried to their places on stage, Kai leaned over to Marina. "After our soft opening for friends and family, we'll have a few days to work out any kinks. So the next week, I've arranged an official opening night for theater reviewers and critics to generate publicity."

Marina frowned. "Do you think inviting critics is wise? They usually review elaborate productions, and this is a fairly amateur cast."

"Carol Reston is our headliner as the incomparable Ghost of Christmas Present," Kai replied, waving her finger in the air. "Plus, they get *moi*," she added with a flourish. "Amateur? I think not! Everyone will rise to the occasion. Besides, we need the publicity."

Kai was performing as the Ghost of Christmas Past, and she wore a shimmering, icicle-white mermaid-style dress with a cascading wig of silvery-white hair, as Dickens had described in the book. Her makeup was sparkly-white with electric-blue eyes, and she wore a crown of glittery seashells.

Marina laughed. Kai was in high spirits tonight. "Do you think the cast is ready?"

"More than ready." Kai rested a hand on Marina's shoulder. "Trust the creative process—we've done the work. Now everything will come together like magic on opening night. It always happens when the spotlight flicks on."

Axe appeared behind them and wrapped Kai in an amiable bear hug. "That's because our fearless director has been a guiding light, shimmering brighter than all of us."

Kai flung her arms around Axe and kissed his cheek. "And here's the man who made all this possible."

Marina watched how easily Kai and Axe interacted with each other. The large man from Montana with the deep voice and cowboy boots couldn't have been more different from Dmitri, Kai's former fiancé, yet he seemed ideal for Kai. They both had a deep love of entertaining, spreading joy, and bringing out the best in others.

Summer Beach needed that.

"Group hug," Kai said, drawing Marina into the circle.

Marina laughed. She needed this, too. Perhaps her sister was right; things often had a way of magically working out—such as her cafe.

With the right amount of hard work behind the scenes, of course.

"The Seashell is the beginning of a new legacy in Summer Beach," Axe said, beaming. "I couldn't have brought this dream to fruition without Kai. I might have planted the seeds, but she brought the sunshine."

"And occasionally the rain clouds," Kai said as they laughed together.

"Nature needs that, too," Marina said. As Axe kissed Kai's forehead, Marina's heart melted for them. "What's the old saying to wish you luck?" All she remembered was that wishing actors luck was considered bad luck.

In unison, Kai and Axe said, "Break a leg!"

"And what does that mean?"

"There are several theories about that," Axe explained. "In the Elizabethan era, audiences would stamp their feet or pound their chair on the floor in approval. If they banged the chair hard enough, they could break a chair leg, which was considered the highest form of appreciation for the play. However, some argue it was the Ancient Greeks, and still others attribute the saying to receiving payment for a performance. Wherever or however the phrase originated, it's an old thespian superstition. Just don't wish us—"

"Shh!" Kai said, admonishing him. "And whatever you do, no mention of that classic Scottish play either."

Marina tilted her head. "Do you mean Mac—"

Kai clamped a hand over Marina's mouth. "We're deadly serious about that one—and I do mean deadly." She turned to Axe. "Now, it's time. Off with you."

After another kiss on her cheek, Axe stepped on stage for his first scene.

Kai gazed after him and smiled.

"Axe is quite a guy," Marina said.

"Isn't he the best?" Kai sighed happily. "I thought that

working together might be the death of our relationship, but it's brought us even closer. It's as if we're breathing the same air, and I feel more like me when I'm with him." She hesitated and dropped her voice to a whisper. "He might really be the one."

"I'll support you on that," Marina said, hugging her sister. She thought highly of the large man with a big heart.

"And what about you and Cole?" Kai asked, inclining her head toward Cole, who was also dressed in his beach-wear costume and waiting in the wings across from them.

"We'll always be good friends," Marina said. That much was true. Whether or not their friendship would develop into something more, she couldn't say. Yet just when she thought of keeping Cole in the friend category, she wondered if she would be missing an opportunity with one of the best men she'd ever known—besides Stan, of course.

As she glanced across the stage, Jack and Leo took their places in the opposite wings. The two grinned and gave her a thumbs-up.

Marina returned the sentiment.

"I heard the odds are back in Cole's favor now," Kai whispered as she watched the exchange. "This should be an interesting holiday season."

"Not you, too?" Marina made a face, yet her heart and her head were out of sync. "Why can't I keep everyone out of my love life?"

"So, you admit that you have a love life." Kai chuckled. "I knew it. Which one is the lucky guy?" She feigned shock with a hand to her mouth. "Or is it both of them?"

"You're incorrigible," Marina said, laughing off her

comment. Fluttering her lashes, she added, "Ginger says a lady never tells."

"That's true," Ginger said, waltzing by with her cape flaring around her. "But tonight, this lady is going to tell everyone a marvelous story."

Taking her spot downstage, Ginger perched on a stool. She would read the narration as if it were a story in an oversized book prop entitled, *A Christmas Carol...At the Beach.* Ginger insisted on memorizing her lines. Jack had illustrated the cover, along with posters they were selling to raise money for the theater.

Marina had to admit Jack was talented. She looked out over what Kai called the house, though it was only benches under a starry night sky.

Brooke's husband and other local firefighters had pitched in to help Axe's construction team build sturdy benches for the audience. They would upgrade the seating in the future, but this was better than people sitting on the cold ground. As Axe often said, they would build this theater brick by brick. It might take time to get everything they wanted, but they were earning their way.

"Places, everyone," Kai called out again, clapping her hands. "Here we go—the final dress rehearsal before opening night." She cued the technical team for lights, and the conductor signaled her little orchestra.

Marina joined her group of extras. They were all eager to begin.

All at once, the magic of the season unfolded around them to the opening chords of *Little Saint Nick* by the Beach Boys on an incredible sound system. Since this wasn't the traditional play but one with a beach twist, Kai and Axe had added beach-inspired tunes. Through Carol and Hal, they'd received permission to use contemporary songs, but they'd also rewritten lyrics to older holiday classics that were now in the public domain.

On stage, Marina joined the opening group of extras. They were playing families bustling through the beach village. Palm trees trimmed in lights sparkled overhead. Marina smiled as she played her brief part.

Next, a spotlight illuminated Jack as Bob Cratchit, shivering against the cold as he worked over a surfboard, and Axe as Scrooge bent over a desk checking his accounting ledgers.

Ginger began to read. "On a wintry Christmas Eve at the beach, poor Bob Cratchit is toiling late at Surfboards by Scrooge & Marley, while Ebenezer Scrooge is counting his money." She motioned to the audience. "Join us now for a magical holiday experience as we visit them on a very special Christmas journey."

Jack crept to a corner to put another lump of coal into the fireplace, but Axe shook his head and bellowed, "Don't be wasteful, Cratchit. It's not even snowing on the beach yet."

"Yes, sir." Jack scurried back to work and pulled the sleeves of his tattered sweatshirt over shivering fingers. He peered up at the clock above him, marking his time.

Mitch from Java Beach strode onto the stage as Scrooge's nephew Fred. Filled with good cheer, he spoke in a strong, clear voice with a hint of surfer dude attitude. "Merry Christmas, Uncle. Will you be joining us for Christmas dinner tomorrow?"

"Bah, humbug," Axe said, scowling.

After leaving the stage, Marina joined Kai again to watch the show from the front. Her sister caught every movement on stage, her pen poised above a notepad. With lights, music, and costumes, the play came to life. It was even more imaginative than Marina had thought it would be, and the cast ran through the scenes without much incident.

Later, when it was time for a crowd scene of carolers on the beach, Marina made another entrance to *Deck the Halls* —only Kai had changed the words. "Deck the beach with boughs of palm fronds, fa-la-la-la-la, la-la-la-la."

From the audience, Marina could hear laughter from a sparse gathering that included Chip, Mayor Bennett, Ivy, and Carol Reston's husband, Hal.

When Marina exited the stage, Carol winked at her. "Well done," she whispered.

"I didn't do much."

"Every part is important," Carol said.

Kai was up next at the Ghost of Christmas Past. Lifting her chin, she slid into character and emerged onto the stage.

Marina watched her as she guided Scrooge through his ghostly treatment in vignettes from his life. As her voice soared into song, Marina felt chills on her spine, and even Carol watched with a smile. Kai was truly exceptional.

When it was Carol's turn on stage, she burst out in character with the rollicking good nature of the Ghost of Christmas Present. She wore a velvet, forest-green cape trimmed in faux white fur over a sequined catsuit. A matching top hat trimmed with mistletoe and studded with starfish completed the ensemble. Carol and Kai had compiled this outfit from Carol's extensive performance wardrobe.

"Wow, she's spectacular," Marina said.

"Isn't she?" Kai was transfixed. "We're so lucky, but I'm sure glad I don't have to follow her act."

Marina could see Ginger tapping her toe, enjoying the musical numbers.

In the next scene, the scary Ghost of Christmas Future didn't say a word, only pointed to a dire future unless Scrooge changed his ways. Brother Rip, the surfing pastor who tended to his beach flock down the beach, played the part to perfection in dark robes with his flowing dreadlocks and a charred oar as a staff. He didn't have to memorize any words, only stage directions, but he brought a serious presence to the role.

Behind her, Leo fidgeted, waiting for his cue.

"You're doing great," Marina said. He'd stolen the scene in his flannel pajamas earlier, and the Christmas dinner scene at the Cratchit home was next.

Taking his position in the wing, Jack grinned at her. "Having fun?"

"This is the best," she said.

"We missed that walk," he said, touching her hand. "Can we get a cup of cocoa after the show?"

"I have to clean up back here. We have a lot to do before the show."

"What if I help?"

Despite her better judgment, Marina nodded. "Okay."

A minute later, Jack shone on stage in Bertrand's red dinner jacket, and Leilani whirled among the children in Ginger's red polka dot dress. The effect was beautiful, yet Marina couldn't take her eyes off Jack. She pressed her hand to her heart, watching him. His performance as Bob Cratchit was nothing short of inspiring, and her eyes misted as she watched.

Just then, Cole stepped beside her and slid his arm around her shoulder. Marina smiled up at him.

To his credit, Cole didn't mention Jack. "Leilani is really good in this scene," he whispered.

With her heart splintering between the two men, Marina could only nod.

15

*J*ack waited at Spirits & Vine, the only spot where they could talk that was still open at this time in the village. The rehearsal had gone fairly well, but now he sat practicing a much tougher role—what he was going to say to Marina.

The stage didn't scare him but entrusting his heart to Marina did. He motioned to a waiter.

"May I have two hot cocoas?" Jack asked.

"We have plenty of holiday editions this year," the waiter replied, ticking them off on his fingers. "Peppermint mocha, spicy Mexican hot chocolate, and pumpkin-spice cocoa. If you like dessert in your cup, we have red velvet hot cocoa. Or, for extra warmth, we're serving cocoa with a shot of Irish cream or hot buttered rum."

Marina slid into the seat across from him. "That last one sounds yummy," she said, sweeping her highlighted brown hair over her shoulder. Her eyes still shimmered with excitement from the rehearsal. "I'm not driving."

"I walked, too," Jack said. The Seashell was within

walking distance of the village, and he lived just on the other side. "Two hot buttered rums," he told the waiter.

"It feels good to relax after the show," Marina said, blowing out a breath.

As she shrugged out of her jacket, Jack couldn't take his eyes off her graceful motions. Still, Jack could tell she was nervous by the way she fidgeted with a fingernail. How had they gotten to this stage when they'd started off so much better?

Unfortunately, he knew the answer to that. The ball had been in his court, and he'd botched his shot. He'd been evasive with her and left her to wonder about his intentions.

One day when he was working with Ginger, the older woman had gone right to the point after finishing one of her stories. *You must always act on what is in your heart. Follow your passion.*

He thought she'd been talking about his illustrations and writing until she added, *And that goes for the special people in your life, too.* She'd given him such a stern look there was no guessing about what she meant.

How did Ginger know him better than he knew himself?

Marina waggled her fingers to get his attention. "You wanted to talk?"

"Sure." Jack shifted in his chair. There was still a lively crowd in the restaurant and bar, but he'd asked for a seat in a quieter section. "It's about Leo."

If there had been a smidgeon of hope in Marina's eyes, it faded now. Not that she wasn't crazy about Leo—Jack knew she was—but she might have hoped they still had a chance.

Otherwise, why would she have come?

At least, that's what Jack liked to think. He ran a hand through his hair. Thankfully, the server interrupted with their drink order.

Jack thanked the waiter. Making small talk, he asked, "Are you coming to the show at the Seashell?"

He felt Marina's eyes on him. She knew he was stalling.

"I hear it's going to be great."

After talking for a couple of minutes, the waiter left them, and Marina tried again.

"You wanted to talk about Leo?"

"Yeah, but more than that, too." At his words, he saw her stiffen. "Just hear me out. I know it's late, and we've had a long day, but it seems like we've been running in different directions all summer doing what we had to do. Me with Leo, you with the cafe. Still, I know those aren't excuses."

Marina shook her head. "That's our reality, isn't it?"

"I'd planned for us to spend more time together—just us, as we'd talked about. Somehow, the summer got away from me. After I'd let you down, it became even harder for me to ask you out."

Her gaze bore into his. "I find this hard to believe coming from a man who would go to the ends of the earth to chase down a story."

"Professional rejection I can handle." He folded a napkin, then folded it again. "I guess I was afraid of being rejected by you."

Marina sipped her hot buttered rum and seemed to think about what he'd said, chewing a corner of her lip. Finally, she asked, "So, should we try again?"

Jack reached for her hand, hardly daring to believe that he had a tiny opening with her. "I'd like nothing more," he said, searching her eyes for validation. "But there's more."

"Leo?"

"Actually, it's Vanessa. She's met someone she's very much interested in."

"After all she's been through with her health, isn't that good?" Marina seemed happy for Vanessa.

Jack knew they'd become friends after the Taste of Summer Beach that Marina had organized. "He's in the medical field, but he doesn't live nearby. Not even in this country."

Marina's smile faded. "How is that going to work?"

Passing a hand over his forehead, Jack said, "To begin with, she and Leo will spend Christmas there."

"That's so soon. But what about Leo and his part in the show?"

"She decided to let him enjoy it for a little while. Another boy will have to take his part. Probably Logan." Jack took a gulp of his warm cocktail. "She hasn't told him yet."

A look of realization filled Marina's face. "That must be what Denise almost let slip the other day."

Jack nodded. "The relationship is serious. Vanessa will look for an apartment over the holidays for them to live." He stared out the window, still trying to come to grips with what this meant. "Leo will be devastated."

Marina smoothed her hand over his. "This will be difficult on you, too. That's quite a distance from Leo."

Jack sucked in a breath and stopped short. His chest constricted as he prepared to tell her his idea. "It won't be that far."

Marina cocked her head. "Are you going, too?"

Jack nodded as he sought to control his emotions. "Since we haven't much more time, I have something to tell you before I leave." He traced her hand with his finger as he spoke. "I have come to care for you more than I ever thought possible. Summer Beach had become my unexpected little heaven on earth. Here I found new work with Ginger, a crazy dog, and a beautiful beach. And then I fell for you, and Leo came into my life. I had everything I could ever want right here."

"And then Vanessa whisks away the most important element." Frowning, Marina twined her fingers with his.

"I need to stay with Leo. I've missed so much of his life. I can work almost anywhere now, and I'd be returning to meet with Ginger fairly often, too. When I'm here, I would be here for you, too." He cleared his throat. "If you think we could make it work."

Marina pressed her lips together in thought. "I don't know…"

Jack tucked her hand firmly in his and brought it to his lips. "You're in my heart, Marina. I was a fool for not taking us seriously enough." And a little scared, he admitted to himself. "I won't make that mistake again."

She squeezed his hand. "Where will you spend most of your time?"

"I'll stay in Europe while Leo is in school to keep helping as I have been." Jack hesitated, calculating the time. "I'd like to spend part of the summer break with him, too. But if Vanessa and Noah take a trip with Leo, I'll be free then. I can return here maybe once a quarter for a week or two depending on Leo's schedule." Even as he said it, his hopes fell.

Disappointment grew in Marina's eyes. "That's not much."

"I might come more often. I just don't know right now."

Marina slid her hand away and cradled the mug like a security blanket. She took a breath. "Like you said, you need to be with Leo." As she drained her mug, he noticed her hand was shaking. Her eyes darted toward the exit as if she was looking for an escape.

Panic seized him. He was losing her. Leaning forward, he said, "Marina, I love you. I have from the moment I first saw you hobbling around the inn."

"Don't remind me." Squeezing her eyes shut, she shook her head and pushed her mug away. "Jack, I can't let you do this to me. You're ripping my heart to shreds, and I don't know what to think anymore." She began to rise.

Desperate now, Jack clutched her arm. "Please, don't go. We still have Christmas. I won't go until after the new year."

"This will be my first holiday with all my family—my children, my sisters and their children, and Ginger. I've been looking forward to having such happy times." She choked back a sob. "I can't let myself be broken up over you, Jack. You have to let me go."

Jack let his hand slide from her. He'd lost her. And probably to Cole. A searing pain seized his chest. Still, he had to give it his best shot. "You can't deny you have feelings for me—and Leo. Can't we try to make this work?"

"We've already tried, and don't you dare use Leo like that." Marina picked up her purse. "Have a Merry Christmas, Jack."

As Jack watched her go, he felt his world implode like a slow-motion movie reel. She was the hope for a future that had anchored his sanity all summer. The vision of a home with her and Leo dissolved in his mind.

Jack clenched his jaw. As soon as the show wrapped, he

would leave. Without Marina, he had no reason to stay in Summer Beach.

He signaled the waiter for the check. While he waited, he sipped his drink. He couldn't avoid his thoughts now.

At the heart of any decision was Leo—the one too young to decide for himself. What was best for him?

The love of devoted parents, of course. Vanessa had made her decision, and now he was left to deal with the fall-out. In fairness, she had been carrying the responsibility for a long time, even though it had been her decision. He hadn't had a choice.

When the waiter brought the bill, Jack paid it and left. Opting to take the quiet beach path home, Jack stared out to the endless sea, considering the constant ebb and flow of the waves, much like the peaks and vicissitudes of life.

A feeling of hopelessness washed over him, and he wished he could find another way.

16

"*O*pening night, let's go," Kai called out.

Marina was touching up her makeup backstage. She'd found the perfect shade of red lipstick to go with a vivid red dress printed with palm trees. A vivid green scarf kept her neck warm. All around her, cast members were jostling for space in front of the mirrors, but spirits were high. After dealing with Jack, this was exactly what she needed. Surely, she could avoid him tonight.

Next to her, Shelly sang out, "Woo-hoo! Let's do this."

Even the usually grumpy Darla joined the cheer, wearing a smile emboldened with cherry red lipstick.

Kai and Axe had invited family and friends for the soft launch at the Seashell. They'd also distributed complimentary tickets to the school for teachers and students to attend. Opening night would be a friendly, low-pressure event to calm jittery nerves.

Next week was the official grand opening of the Seashell and the debut of the holiday show. As Marina slid a tube of lipstick into her bag, she thought about Leo. The boy's mother still hadn't told him about their change of holiday plans. On one hand, Marina understood that Vanessa wanted him to enjoy the show as long as he could, but on the other, she was springing a life-changing decision on him at the last moment.

That wasn't any of Marina's business, but she couldn't help feeling sorry for Leo. Especially since he loved being in the show. He'd found his place and made a lot of friends.

Marina left the dressing room along with others who were eager to begin. As she was walking toward the wings, Ginger signaled to her.

"I've forgotten my lipstick at home, dear. What I'm wearing seems to disappear so quickly. May I use yours to freshen up?"

"Come with me," Marina said. "I'll apply it for you with a brush like I used to do on set. That will last longer under stage lights."

"Just as long as those lights are warm," Ginger said, rubbing her hands together. A chill had blown in from the ocean that afternoon.

Going against the flow of cast members streaming from the dressing room, Marina slid through the crowd and toward the now deserted dressing area. "Have a seat," she said with a flourish. "Your makeup artist is in."

Marina had done her own makeup for the news broadcast for years, so she had learned to apply foundation that didn't create a shine, eye makeup that looked soft on camera, and lipstick that would last through entire news shows or interviews.

"I feel so pampered," Ginger said, tilting her face to her granddaughter.

Marina had always enjoyed helping her grandmother. As she cleaned the old lipstick from her face, she noticed the lines around Ginger's lips had become a little more pronounced. However, they were nothing she couldn't smooth out with her special arsenal of products.

As she prepped the lip area to keep lipstick from bleeding, she thought about Ginger, who had always seemed ageless to her. Ginger had been in her prime for decades—and she still was.

Yet, Marina had to be realistic. She didn't know how much longer Ginger would remain vibrant, but she could resolve to make every day special for her grandmother. Someday, Marina might not get a second chance to tell Ginger how much she loved her. So she would do it now and every day.

Marina took a step back to assess the look. "Well, hello gorgeous. Let's put on the paint now." Reaching into her bag, she brought out her lipstick brush, liner, and bold red lipstick.

Ginger coughed into her hand. "Just a moment," she said, coughing again." My throat has been a little scratchy. You wouldn't happen to have any lozenges in that bag?"

"I'll find some for you." Even if she had to send someone out to get them. Marina didn't like the sound of that cough.

Ginger cleared her throat. "Now, I'm ready. While you're doing this, I want to hear the latest development with Jack."

"Why do you think I'd know anything about him?" Marina tried to keep her hand steady as she outlined Ginger's still strong lip line.

When Marina finished, Ginger said, "The way you're

both moping around tonight? A simple deduction, my dear. The holidays can be a time of stress, but I suspect there is something more."

"Actually, it has to do with Vanessa and Leo." Marina told her about Vanessa's plan as she cleaned her brush.

"I see," Ginger said thoughtfully. "And where does Cole figure into this equation?"

Marina glanced over her shoulder. They were still alone. "He's a good man," she said carefully.

"That's not what I asked. Let me make this clear for you." She went on while Marina dabbed her brush over the lipstick. "From what you've told me, you have a friend who wants to be a lover—and a lover who wants to be a friend." Ginger tapped her fingers together. "Does that sum it up?"

"Fairly well, I'm afraid," Marina said.

"Are you sure you have all the facts?"

Marina sighed. She was hesitant to tell Ginger about Jack's profession of love for her at Spirits & Vine. It was simply too painful to repeat.

Ginger watched her closely while Marina worked. Her grandmother had always been able to tell when something was troubling her.

"Never mind what they want," Ginger said when Marina paused. "What's missing in the equation is what you desire. You're in charge, my dear. Choose one—or none. Wait for another whirl on the merry-go-round. In the meantime, you can be perfectly happy by yourself. Forever, if you want."

"I don't care what Jack does with his life," Marina said, determined to convince herself. "Besides, the distance would be too great."

Ginger pursed her lips in the mirror. "Bertrand often

traveled on government business, and later, so did I. That made the time we had together more special. I'd even go so far as to say spectacular." A small smile played on Ginger's mouth as her eyes glazed with happy memories.

"I don't know how that would work."

"You could visit Jack when the cafe is slow in the winter months," Ginger said. "Switzerland is so lovely then. What a grand adventure you could have. If that's what you wanted."

Marina had acted decisively last night with Jack, but had she acted too quickly? Ginger brought up a possibility Marina hadn't even considered.

As the thought that she'd missed a possible alternative gnawed at her, she brushed lipstick on Ginger's lips, blotted, powdered, and added a touch of gloss for sheen. Stepping back to admire her handiwork, Marina said, "There. That will last all night. And I'll have throat lozenges or another solution for you at the end of the first act."

Ginger rose and hugged her carefully so as not to damage their hair and makeup. "I'm glad we had this talk. You'll never regret doing what's in your heart—that, I guarantee."

"Thank you for reminding me." Marina held her grandmother. "I love you so much, Ginger. You've always been my rock."

"I love you, too, Marina." Ginger gazed at her with pride in her eyes. "And remember, when the path is right, you'll know it."

. . .

ON HER WAY TO join Kai and Axe for the pre-opening pep talk, Marina saw a stagehand she'd heard was a healthcare practitioner by day. She explained Ginger's ailment.

"I don't have anything on me," the woman said. "But she should gargle with saltwater or drink honey and ginger tea."

"We have all of that backstage," Marina said. Brooke had brought drinks and snacks for the cast and crew. She'd prepare something for Ginger. "Say, aren't you new to Summer Beach?"

The woman nodded. "I'm Bettina. My husband and I just moved here. We vacationed in Summer Beach and fell in love with it."

Marina smiled. "I'm fairly new myself. We can talk at the after-party, but we'd better join the rest of the cast."

They hurried toward the group gathered backstage.

"Gather in," Kai said to everyone. "This is just like the dress rehearsal, only with a few more people we know in the audience."

"A lot more," someone said, and others laughed.

Marina gave her sister a thumbs-up. Tonight was the culmination of Kai's long-held dreams of writing and directing. And to direct Carol Reston was more than she'd ever imagined; Carol had taught her a lot as well.

Kai's eyes shimmered with excitement as she passed the floor to Carol.

"Tonight, let's all go out there and have fun entertaining everyone," Carol said, standing in costume next to Kai. "Remember, this crowd loves you and wants to support you."

"I'm nervous because all our friends are out there," one woman said, chewing on a fingernail. "What if I mess up?"

Darla frowned, adding, "I hope I don't make a darn fool of myself."

"Like Carol said, relax and have fun," Kai said. "Opening night jitters are normal, but you were all marvelous at the rehearsal. Know you can do it, and pour your heart into it."

"Good luck, everyone," Darla said.

"No!" Kai exclaimed, holding up her palms. "Never do that—it's bad luck for actors."

"That's only a superstition," Axe said quickly. Then, cheering everyone on, he added, "Let's all break a leg tonight."

Marina laughed at their antics. Still, she felt a little unnerved, although she wasn't sure why. She was glad she was an extra and wouldn't have a spotlight on her.

She glanced around. Everyone seemed ready. Ginger stood in the wings, waiting to go on and open the show.

Marina slid a look at Jack. As always, he looked confident, though he wore a serious expression as if he were already slipping into character. Still, he had a hand on Leo's shoulder, reassuring him.

Ginger's words played in her mind. Which would she regret more—walking away from Jack or Cole?

Or not choosing either one of them?

She shook tension from her hands. Now was not the time to think about major life decisions. *Live in the moment,* she told herself.

Closing her eyes, she listened to a musician softly tuning an instrument and chatter from the audience. On the cool ocean breeze, she could smell briny freshness, along with a hint of apple cider that Brooke was serving. Her sister had managed all the picnic box reservations and distribution.

Feeling more grounded, Marina opened her eyes. Jack swiftly turned away. Had he been watching her?

She couldn't think about that. Instead, she turned her attention to other actors hurrying to their places. The conductor lifted her baton, the music began, and the show was underway.

The performance began just as it had before, and Marina breathed a sigh of relief for Kai.

A little too soon, as it turned out.

In the first scene, Jack forgot a line, although Axe covered for him. A little later, Leo nearly fell out of bed. Jack caught him, but Leo stammered through his next line. Marina's heart went out to them.

"No one noticed," Marina whispered to Kai, who was looking worried. However, even Kai made a mistake in her first song.

Kai made a face. "This is what happens when someone wishes us you-know-what."

"You don't really believe that." Marina knew her sister would be harder on herself than anyone else. Kai was a professional, after all. But as she'd once told her, even pros make mistakes.

Thinking about the on-set disaster that ended her career, Marina could relate. The audience would quickly forget the error—unless, of course, it became an international meme shared millions of times on social media.

Surely, like lightning, that would rarely strike twice. Lifting her chin, Marina stepped toward her entry spot, ready to go on after Jack and Leo and Leilani finished their scene.

Just then, as Leilani exited the stage, she tripped and

fell, careening headfirst into the wings. Jack rushed to help her up, but Leilani collapsed as soon as she tried to put weight on her foot. Vehemently, she shook her head.

"I can't," Leilani whispered, tears springing to her eyes.

Kai and the stagehand Marina had spoken to earlier knelt beside her.

"I'm a nurse," Bettina said softly. "I'll look after her and get her the help she needs." She began to inspect Leilani's ankle.

"Thank you," Kai whispered. Turning to Marina, she held up her hand. "Wait a minute."

Marina took a step back from the stage. "But I'm in this scene."

"I might need you," Kai said, biting her lip.

Wincing against the pain, Leilani tried to put pressure on her foot but couldn't. She looked at Kai with sorrow in her eyes and shook her head. "I think I've sprained or broken my ankle. I'm so sorry."

Bettina looked at Kai and nodded. "There's no way she can go on with the show tonight. I need to get ice on this for her right away."

"It's okay," Kai said, her voice rich with compassion. "These things happen." Quickly, she shifted into her action mode, checking the notated script on her clipboard. "Marina, I need you to step into the role of Mrs. Cratchit."

"But I don't know that part," Marina said, shocked at the suggestion. And of all the roles, that of Jack's wife was the last she would have wanted.

Balancing on one foot and leaning against Bettina, Leilani appealed to her. "You can do it. Jack will help you."

Looking uncomfortable with the idea, Jack swiftly averted his gaze.

With her pulse hammering, Marina turned her back to Jack. "Kai, please—isn't there someone else?"

Her sister shook her head. "There's a big scene right before that one. No one will have time for a costume change before the next scene with Mrs. Cratchit. You've watched this a dozen times in rehearsal. Come on, Marina. Everyone needs you to step up now."

17

*M*arina's head throbbed at the thought of acting opposite Jack, and she felt a little dizzy at how quickly everything was happening. But Kai and the rest of the cast needed her.

Taking a deep breath, Marina turned to Jack. "Okay. Show me what to do."

For a moment, Jack looked as shocked as she felt, but then he nodded and sprang into action. "We have time while the ghosts of Christmas enlighten Scrooge."

"And I'm up next," Kai said. "Jack, please run lines with Marina. And let's have Leilani's husband help Leilani to a dressing room. Here he comes now."

Roy Miyake hurried to Leilani. While he helped his wife to a dressing room, Kai turned to Marina. "Thank you," she whispered, hugging her. "Got to go."

As Kai slipped into character and strode on stage, regaling the crowd, Marina realized what a responsibility her sister had taken on. Despite Marina's feelings toward Jack, she wouldn't let Kai down.

"I'll bring Leo," Jack said. "He's in that scene, too."

They hurried to the small dressing room where Marina had helped Ginger with her makeup. With Kai's vocals soaring on stage, Jack pulled his script from his bag.

Leaning toward her, he showed her the part of Mrs. Cratchit, and Marina quickly reviewed it.

"This is so cool," Leo said, grinning. "You'll be my stage mom. That means you'll be married to my dad in the show."

Jack shifted uncomfortably on a stool. "I never thought—"

"Neither did I," Marina said, feeling her cheeks flaming. "Let's just do this."

"Okay." Jack tapped the script. "First, when I come home, you'll embrace me."

She sighed. "I remember that part." She held out her arms and gave him a stiff hug.

Jack pulled away. "We're going to have to do better than that."

"I will…we will," she stammered. "What's next?"

"You check the small turkey in the oven."

"Right." She made the motions. "Next line?"

Just then, her friend Ivy tapped on the doorjamb. She held the red polka dot dress in her arms. "I hate to interrupt, but here's Leilani's costume for that scene. She suggested you change while you rehearse."

"That's where I draw the line," Marina said, throwing a look at Jack.

He handed Ivy his script and put his arm around Leo. "Keep it going while she changes. We'll be right outside the door. She has to memorize that fast."

As Ivy shut the door, Marina was already stepping out of her shoes. "Looks like Leilani and I wear almost the same size." However, Leilani was slimmer, just as Ginger had been when she wore the dress. Marina hoped she could zip it.

While she changed, Ivy read the script to her.

"Can you help me with this zipper?" Marina asked, turning around.

"Take a deep breath," Ivy replied, trying to slide the zipper. After working on it, she passed a hand over her forehead. "I can't close it over the waistline."

"We have to." Marina spied a wide belt hanging over the back of a chair. It was an extra's who'd decided not to wear it. Darla, if she recalled correctly, whose waistline was more like hers. Marina dug a pair of scissors from her bag. "Slit the side seams at the waist. I can cover it with a belt and cape."

Ivy smiled with relief. "Hang on half a minute." After snipping threads in the seams at the waistline, she zipped up the dress and wrapped the belt around her. Standing back, she smiled. "Wow, that worked. You look great."

"You'd be surprised what I did to make outfits work in a bind on the air," Marina said, hugging her. "Thank goodness you're here."

Ivy grinned. "You can do this. And you'll have one of Shelly's Sea Breeze cocktails waiting for you after the show."

"I'm going to need it. Now, I'd better get Jack back in here." Marina gave a wry smile. She'd confided in Ivy, her old friend from their teenage years. "I never thought I'd say that."

"We'll have a good story for later," Ivy said, consoling

her. "For the record, I think you're pretty brave, especially considering the circumstances." She opened the door.

Marina worked on the scene with Jack and Leo for a little longer before the stage manager tapped on the door. "You're up soon. Let's go."

Jack folded his script and put it away. "I'm here for you. Don't worry. There's nothing you can do up there that I can't get us out of—one way or another." He held his hand out to her.

"You can believe that," Leo said. "I almost fell out of bed in that last scene, but Dad caught me." He looked up at Jack with admiration in his eyes. "And I'll be there to help you, too."

"That makes me feel better." Marina hugged Leo. Although Jack might have been remiss in the boyfriend department, she had to give him credit in the Dad division. He really loved Leo. She took the boy's hand.

"Let's do this." Marina gave a strangled laugh and slid her other hand into Jack's. His grip was warm and sure, and she had to trust him.

The three of them set off for the stage.

"Break a leg," Kai whispered. "I'll feed you lines if you need them."

Marina nodded. At least she was accustomed to that from her broadcasting experience. However, it had been a long time since her last disastrous on-air appearance. She wished she had an earpiece.

As the stagehands executed a scene change, Jack led Marina on stage. "Trust me," he whispered.

While her nerves did the cha-cha, Marina calmly looked out over the audience. Many people had dressed up in holiday garb for opening night. She took a breath; she had to do this—even with Jack's presence still channeling serious signals to her overloaded psyche.

The scene opened with her and the children, then Jack made his entrance. He and Marina embraced. In his arms, her heart thudded and she felt light-headed. She struggled to maintain her composure, though she felt it slipping.

She could see people in the front row mentioning her name and pointing, but to Jack's credit, he carried the action smoothly. Still, his presence threw her off. Backstage with others around was one thing, but here on stage, with the spotlight on her, she couldn't take her eyes off his.

Tearing herself from him, Marina crossed to the painted plywood oven and removed a paper mache turkey, bobbling it as she did.

However, as she placed the platter on the table, she couldn't remember the next line, which infuriated her. She'd had professional training for live appearances, but this wasn't scripted news or a planned interview—and Jack hadn't been on the set making her nervous.

She couldn't freeze. And yet, she did.

When in doubt, say something plausible. Marina blurted out, "Did you invite Scrooge for dinner?"

"Scrooge?" Jack, in his role as Bob Cratchit, turned to her with a grin. "Only my lovely wife would have it in her heart to invite Mr. Scrooge for our holiday dinner."

Marina still couldn't recall the next line. Kai was mouthing something, but in the glare of the lights, Marina couldn't understand her. Worse, her throat was closing up. She bustled around the table, feeling her cheeks flaming.

"That would be nice if Mr. Scrooge could come," Leo said, his sweet, clear voice ringing out in support of Marina. "Even if some of the kids don't like him."

Marina saw Kai flipping madly through the pages on her clipboard. They were clearly way off the script now.

Marina had to say something again. *Anything.* "Why do people dislike Mr. Scrooge, dear?"

Jack stared at her for a moment.

Now she'd thrown off the entire scene. She was hopelessly lost.

All at once, Jack spun to face the audience. "Why, indeed? I'll tell you why."

With an exaggerated wink, Jack grabbed a pair of spoons from the table and started to slap them together, playing the spoons in rhythm like old-time music as he rapped to the beat.

"A one, a two, a one, two, three, four…
He's odious,
Parsimonious,
That grinch who stole
Our festivus—hey, hey!"

While Jack performed an impromptu solo on the spoons, the conductor and musicians picked up the beat. Marina had to laugh at his silly rhymes and references to Dr. Seuss and the old television series, *Seinfeld.* Fortunately, the crowd roared with laughter, cheering Jack on.

Feeding off that energy, Jack rapped another verse in the *Hamilton* style from Lin-Manuel Miranda while he danced around the dinner table. The children fell in behind him—Leo, Samantha, Logan, and Brooke's boys—circling the table in a conga line like a scene out of *Beetlejuice* with Catherine O'Hara and Michael Keaton.

The audience clapped along with them. Instantly,

Marina's nerves dissipated, and she started enjoying herself. And then, all at once, the lines she'd forgotten popped into her head, although they were no longer relevant.

Catching a glimpse of Kai, Marina saw her sister toss her clipboard aside and raise her hands as if giving up.

While Jack continued his holiday rap, Marina marveled at him. He certainly had a way with words—many different words. Joseph Pulitzer might be turning in his grave, but Marina thought the old newspaper man would somehow find a story in this crazy fiasco.

Jack led them out of the dance with a final salute to Scrooge. They continued the scene, somewhat altered and ad-libbed, but they made it.

As they exited the stage to more applause, Marina clasped hands with Jack and Leo again, feeling like they had triumphed over adversity of her own making.

She knew that it was Jack's silly song that had saved her, although it was likely at his expense. "I'm so grateful to you," she whispered.

"That would only work in Kai's crazy version of *A Christmas Carol*," Jack said, sounding relieved.

"Thank goodness there are no critics in the crowd," she said. Fortunately, Summer Beach was a small village, and Kai had been smart to schedule reviewers the following week for the official opening night. Unless a major publication had sent someone to see Carol Reston perform, they were safe.

Jack touched the small of her back as they made their way backstage. "We'll have time to rehearse before the big opening."

Marina was grateful to Jack, yet she would hate to see

him destroy his professional reputation over this. She knew how that felt.

She would be better prepared for the next performance. No more mistakes, she vowed.

Backstage, Marina and Jack came face to face with Kai.

Her sister jabbed her hands on her hips and glared at them. "And just what do you call that out there?"

18

"Kai, please don't be upset," Marina said. "Jack was covering for me. It was my fault."

All at once, Kai burst out laughing. "It. Was. Genius!" She raised her hands in high-fives to all of them. "That stays in the show." She bumped Jack's shoulder. "We have to work on the lyrics, though. I mean, *festivus*—really? It's Christmas."

Jack grinned, clearly a little embarrassed. "I don't know...the syllables flowed better with the beat or something." He threw up his hands. "It's not like I had more than a split second to think about it, and I'd been watching *Seinfeld* reruns the night before."

"You might have a call for an encore at the party tonight," Kai said, laughing. "See you later." She rushed back to her post.

Several extras, including Cole, paused to congratulate them before taking their places for the next scene.

The lights dimmed and the scene got underway with Carol Reston singing a song she'd written years before. It was about spreading the love and joy of the holiday season every day of the year.

"I love this song," Marina whispered to Jack. The audience was listening in awestruck silence as Carol sang from her heart with real emotion. Marina leaned into Jack, thinking about what the words meant in her life.

He put his arm around her, and without hesitation, she rested her head on his shoulder, blinking back tears of happiness. Swaying to the music in the darkness, they watched as Carol touched the hearts of everyone at the Seashell. The outpouring of love was almost palpable.

Marina didn't know what tomorrow would bring, but tonight, right now, was perfect. While Jack went on stage for another scene, she stayed behind, watching from the wings and thinking about how much she loved her life in Summer Beach.

Even with Jack in the picture. He might be leaving, but at least she discovered that she could deeply care for someone again. Maybe that was the only reason their paths crossed.

In his final happy scene, Leo delivered the last line as Tiny Tim, saying, "God bless us, every one!"

The audience laughed, clapped, and wiped tears of happiness from their eyes as Ginger brought the show to a close with her superb narration. As she did, Santa Claus appeared on stage, waving to all the children.

"Ho, ho, ho! Merry Christmas!" Santa called out.

Marina laughed. Kai had kept Santa's identity a secret until now. It was Bennett Dylan, the mayor of Summer Beach.

Ginger waved back. "And a Merry Christmas to you,

Santa, and to everyone here tonight." She finished with a kiss to the audience and a wave goodbye.

The audience—the friends and families of the cast and crew—sprang to their feet, clapping and cheering for their loved ones.

Backstage, Jack took Marina's hand. "Let's take a bow, Mrs. Cratchit."

Laughing, Marina raced on stage with him and took her bow. And then, turning to the wings, she motioned for Leilani.

With her husband Roy and Cole helping her out, Leilani waved to the audience, who applauded her spirit and performance.

At last, Carol joined them all on stage. With hands clasped, they took a group bow before enthusiastic applause and cheers.

Despite the near disaster, Marina couldn't remember when she'd had so much fun. And Jack still held her hand. She glanced around to see where Cole might be, but he'd disappeared right after the final curtain call.

Axe joined them, a smile on his face. "Way to play those spoons," he said, punching Jack in the arm. "Where'd you learn that?"

Jack grinned and ran a hand through his hair. "At an old country bar back in Texas. We were kids and didn't have much to amuse ourselves. A couple of old-timers taught me how to play the spoons—the harmonica and washboard, too."

"A washboard?" Axe chuckled. "I'll keep that in mind for a future show. Do you have any other hidden talents?"

Jack glanced at Marina. "Besides a talent for getting out of scrapes?"

Kai hugged Marina. "Things always work out, some-times even better than we'd planned. That's the genius of creativity."

At that, Ginger turned to them. "I believe that's what I've always told you, Kai. I'm glad to know you were listening after all."

"My sisters and I have heard every word of wisdom you've dispensed, even if we're a little slow to put it into action." Kai hugged her grandmother. "You were magnifi-cent, by the way. How is your cough?"

"Bettina looked after me during intermission, and I felt much better in the second half. Old remedies are often the best—as long as one tends to the problem early." Ginger smiled at Marina and Jack. "And you two were certainly a hit with the audience. Jack, you're a man full of surprises—you must share your gifts more often."

"That was thanks to Marina tonight," he said, squeezing her hand.

"Very funny," Marina replied, but she enjoyed joking with him. He'd saved the scene—and perhaps the entire play.

After a short meeting of the cast and crew, everyone made their way to the Coral Cafe, where Brooke and Chip had set up a buffet for the opening night party. They'd finished the holiday decorations Marina had started putting up, and the entire patio glowed with fairy lights. Pine cones decorated the tables, and the fir branches Marina had collected in the mountains and fashioned into wreaths hung by red ribbons.

As the cast and crew began to arrive, happy chatter and laughter filled the air. People posed for photos and signed the playbill for the cast that Kai had printed.

Marina knew or recognized almost everyone there from rehearsals, except for a tall, lean man in black-rimmed glasses who stood alone, scribbling in a small spiral notebook. She made her way toward him.

"Hello, I'm Marina Moore. Is there anything I can get for you?"

The man frowned. "You work here?"

She swept her hand across the patio. "It's my cafe."

He pointed his pen toward her as if accusing her of an evil deed. "You were also in the show."

"That's right," she said, bristling at his attitude.

"You took the place of the other actor in the part of Mrs. Cratchit."

"Right again."

"You were definitely not her regular understudy."

"Well, no, but—"

"That will probably be rectified." He pushed his glasses up on his nose and made a note. "Marina Moore..." He paused and studied her. "Why does your name sound familiar?"

"I don't think we've ever met." Marina didn't dare mention her broadcast work and hoped he wouldn't recall her unfortunate meme. Just as she was growing uncomfortable, Carol Reston waved at her and hurried toward them with her husband, Hal.

"Why, Rexford, darling," Carol said, greeting the man. "I didn't know you were in the audience."

"Just doing my job, Carol."

Hal shook Rexford's hand. "Always good to see you, sport. And I see you've met Marina, who filled in admirably this evening on short notice after an accident. Rexford is a theater critic from Los Angeles."

As her mouth went dry, Marina managed to say, "Nice to meet you."

This wasn't right. Kai had invited critics to next week's official opening. Tonight was meant as a soft launch, and except for professionals like Carol and Kai, most of the actors had been nervous. Marina could just imagine what Rexford might write. He was staring at her, so she added, "The new Seashell is a fine addition to Summer Beach."

Rexford twisted his mouth to one side. "First time I've been here." Studying her face, he snapped his finger. "Say, weren't you the anchorwoman from San Fran—"

"Oh, sorry," Marina cut him off quickly. "I'm being called to the kitchen. Excuse me."

On her way, she grabbed Kai's hand and swept her into the kitchen with her. "That man out there in the dark suit and glasses is a critic," she said.

Kai's mouth dropped open. "He saw the show?"

"And took notes."

Peering out, Kai spotted him and rolled her eyes. "Of all people to come early. That's Rexford Rutherford, who is as snooty as they come. I heard that Rexford and Carol have had a war going on for years."

Marina motioned to Axe to join them. "I wonder who let him in?"

"It wasn't as if we were checking IDs at the door," Kai said. "This is friends-and-family night."

Axe strode into the kitchen. Taking one look at Kai's frown, he said, "What's wrong?"

"We had a critic in the audience tonight," Kai said. "One of the harshest." While Kai told Axe, Marina excused herself to welcome more people.

It was too late now, she supposed. Fortunately, Carol

and Hal were still speaking to Rexford. If anyone could sway a positive review, it would be Carol and Hal. But even superstars received poor reviews. Marina had to put that out of her head tonight.

Leo burst onto the patio, dragging his mother by the hand. "Mom is letting me stay up for the party," he said, still excited from the show.

Vanessa smiled. "It's past his bedtime, but it's just this time, and his friends are here."

"I'm glad you came," Marina said. She had come to know Vanessa through Leo, and she admired the other woman's strength and resolve.

Vanessa's short, dark hair was cropped and curly, making her lovely dark eyes seem even larger. Marina was so glad that Ginger's connections proved fruitful, allowing Vanessa to receive experimental treatment—although Vanessa was still unaware of the connection.

"Samantha, Logan!" Leo called out and raced toward his friends, who were with their parents, too.

Marina laughed. "Leo really helped me through that awkward scene tonight. He's so talented."

"I had no idea he would enjoy performing so much," Vanessa said. "Maybe he takes after his father in that regard."

Marina gazed after the boy. "I understand Leo doesn't know yet, but Jack told me about your plans. I'm so happy that you found someone special."

Vanessa's lips parted in surprise. "I never expected such a wonderful man to come into my life, but Noah is everything I could have wished for. I hope this doesn't complicate Leo's relationship with his father."

"Having Jack in Zurich will help Leo adjust," Marina

said. While she didn't say it, Marina was thinking about what a good father Jack had turned out to be, even though —in his words—he was still in training.

"Jack is planning to move there?" Vanessa's brow shot up.

"For Leo," Marina said. "He'd do anything for his son."

Vanessa seemed genuinely surprised. "I suppose Jack can find work in Europe. He was always in demand." She gazed after Leo. "My son has grown to love Summer Beach, but I thought this would be a new adventure for us."

"You deserve a loving relationship," Marina said. "That doesn't come around often."

"No, it doesn't." Vanessa sighed. "Noah is an incredible man." She brightened. "Maybe you can visit us in Zurich someday. Leo is so fond of you."

"As I am of him." Marina didn't know what else to say. Between her decision to leave Jack, her grandmother's advice, and the connection she and Jack had tonight—her emotions were on a roller-coaster ride. *One day at a time*, she told herself. *Live in the moment.*

Vanessa touched Marina's shoulder and lowered her voice. "Thank you for telling me about Jack's plans." She furrowed her brow. "I didn't realize he cared so much for Leo already. The Jack I knew years ago was quite different."

"He loves Leo very much," Marina said. She saw it in everything Jack did. He had put Leo first in his life. "Jack left New York and changed his career for his son. He was only on a sabbatical when you called him."

"I know my son is lucky to have him," Vanessa said thoughtfully. "Perhaps I shouldn't have waited so long to introduce them."

"Only the future matters now." Marina hesitated. She

wanted to add an observation, even if it wasn't any of her business. There were times in her life when she wished someone had given her an honest opinion. She opened her mouth to speak, but quickly thought better of it. Vanessa might not want to hear it.

"Did you have something else to say?" Vanessa asked.

Marina glanced around. No one was listening to them —only Ginger was nearby—and this would only take a moment. Summoning her courage, she went on. "A truly wonderful, special life must await you and Leo in Zurich for you to leave Summer Beach. It's hard to replace good friends like Denise and John—and Leo will surely miss Samantha. Summer Beach offers such an idyllic childhood for your son, what with good friends and Jack nearby. And Leo said Scout is the first dog he's ever had."

Vanessa smiled. "Leo can have another dog in Switzerland."

"All I'm saying is, it must be hard to leave. I'm sure you've thought all that through or you wouldn't be acting so decisively. Noah must be quite remarkable." She paused, thinking about what Ginger said. "Sometimes, there are alternatives we haven't thought about."

Vanessa raised her brow. "With my illness, I had to be decisive," she said with a defensive edge to her voice. "I couldn't put off things to a tomorrow that might never come." Yet a moment later, she reined in her emotions. "I still don't know how much time I have—I suppose none of us do—but maybe I have been leaping ahead."

"I did that once," Marina said softly, remembering Grady. "It didn't end well."

Vanessa gazed out toward the ocean. "I think you've

been very good for Leo. And Jack. They'll miss you, and I really wish this would have worked out in your favor, too."

Shaking her head, Marina said, "I'm only thinking about your son. I know how hard it was for me in San Francisco to raise my children without a strong support group."

Vanessa nodded thoughtfully. "I wish there was another way, but Noah's work is in Zurich, and he means so much to me."

"Of course, I understand." Marina had done what she could.

"Thank you for sharing your thoughts and concern for Leo, though," Vanessa said, pressing her hand to Marina's arm. With a faint smile, she moved away to speak to Denise and John.

Marina brushed her arms against the evening chill. Maybe Vanessa didn't want to hear her opinion, but Marina really thought this move would be traumatic for Leo. With his mother's illness, he'd already suffered through a difficult period. Summer Beach was the first ray of sunshine he'd had in a long time.

Ginger strolled toward her. "That looked serious."

"It wasn't a conversation I wanted to have at a party, but I can't help wondering if Vanessa is making a mistake. Her new boyfriend might be a wonderful man, but I'd thought that about Grady, too. Taking a little longer to get to know someone can't hurt."

"Women should look out for one another," Ginger said with a nod. "If you'll excuse me, I see our Santa Claus, Mayor Bennett. I need to have a word with him—and for your information, Kai looks like she's ready to dance."

Marina blew out a breath. "I suppose I should enjoy the party." She looked out over the gathering crowd. Thankfully, the theater critic had left before people began to let off their pent-up anxiety from opening night. For Kai's sake, she hoped Rexford would be kind, but regardless, she'd be there to support her.

As Ginger had warned, Kai turned up the music, and people started dancing. They were all having such a good time. At the center of it was Leilani, snapping her fingers to the beat and enjoying herself, even with her foot and ankle elevated and iced.

Marina was glad Leilani had the chance to perform one scene on opening night. No one knew how long Leilani would be out until she'd seen a doctor. After Christmas, she and her husband would take their annual trip to visit family in Hawaii for the winter months, which would be a perfect place for her to heal if her injury was more serious.

At least she was having a good time now, Marina thought. *Living in the moment.*

"Hey you," Kai said, sashaying toward her and clapping her hands. "Come on, let's celebrate. With that long face, you need to dance with us right now."

Marina laughed. "I sure do."

MARINA COULDN'T REMEMBER when she'd danced so much. Kai was still blasting the music, but Marina had to take a break. No longer chilled, she eased into a chair and fanned her face.

"You've got some good moves." Cole handed her a rose-colored cocktail. "Ivy had Shelly prepare this for you. She called it a Sea Breeze Cooler and said you'd earned it."

"Ivy remembered," Marina said, grateful for the cranberry and grapefruit juice cocktail. This was one of her favorites. She waved at Ivy and Shelly across the patio and sipped the cooler.

Cole had changed into a tailored shirt and slacks for the party and looked very nice. "I didn't get a chance to properly congratulate you on your performance."

"That means a lot to me," Marina said. "Have a seat."

"I don't think I could have pulled off what you did," he said, sitting down. "That was quite a scene to remember."

"As it turned out, I forgot the lines," Marina said, tapping her head. "Jack saved the scene by ad-libbing."

Cole chuckled. "I didn't think I'd heard that song before. I would have remembered it."

"Kai wants to keep it in the show. With a little polish, of course."

An earnest expression filled his face. "You and Jack play well opposite each other."

Marina wasn't sure what Cole meant by that. "He helped me rehearse. With his theatrical training, he knew what to do."

"It seemed like more of a connection than that," Cole said thoughtfully. "You and Jack have a history."

"A very short one." Marina wasn't sure where she stood with either man.

Cole thought about this. "After the show, I'll drive back east to see my kids. That offer I made you is still open. Would you like to take that trip with me?"

Marina smiled. "To be honest with you, we don't have that kind of relationship yet."

"That's what I thought you might say. If it helps, that sofa makes into a bed, and I could sleep there." With a note of hope in his voice, he added, "Unless you didn't want me to do that."

"It's thoughtful of you to put it that way." She touched his arm. "I'm not Babs, Cole, and I never will be."

"No one is," he said with a tinge of sadness. "However, I don't want you to think I'm overstepping your boundaries. You still mean a lot to me, Marina. The offer will be open until I leave."

"We have an old connection, Cole. But we should think about that before we do something we might regret."

The tips of Cole's ears reddened with embarrassment. "Maybe I made a fool of myself by showing up here unannounced. Did I overstay my welcome by getting involved in the show?"

"Not at all. Please don't think that. We all enjoy having you in Summer Beach."

Taking her hand, Cole let out a sigh of relief. "These past few weeks have been the best gift I could have imagined. You, Ginger and Kai, and Brooke and Chip, have treated me like part of your family. I haven't had that in a long time because my kids have lives of their own. I'm just old Dad now, like an extra wheel. And Babs was through with me a long time ago." He caught himself and shook his head. "Maybe I shouldn't talk about her so much."

"It's okay. She's the mother of your children."

"And she's been a good one," he said. "Anyway, I haven't decorated for the holidays in years, and I didn't realize how much I missed it. It was a lot of fun."

Marina smiled at him. "Ginger roped you into that, I'm afraid."

"I didn't mind. And being part of this show is amazing. Maybe I should get more involved in community activities. After the divorce, I didn't get out much. But this has been fun, and so is traveling. You'll let me know about the trip?"

"I will." Even though Cole wasn't giving up, she kissed him on the cheek. "Thanks for understanding."

"Actually, I do," Cole said. "And I respect you for that." Just then, his phone buzzed. He took it out and checked it.

"Do you need to answer that?" Marina asked.

"It's Babs." Cole grinned, but he also seemed a little embarrassed. "I told her about the show, and she's thinking about flying out to see it. Although that's probably an excuse to escape an early snowstorm. She must be calling to see how it went."

"Answer it, and tell her hello for me."

As Cole stepped aside to take the call, a thought crossed Marina's mind. She could see him smiling and talking animatedly with his ex-wife. Marina knew they had a connection through their children, though she sensed it went deeper than that.

More than that, Marina still suspected that Babs wasn't happy in her new marriage. She made a mental note to try to reach her again.

Maybe Cole wasn't really available either.

19

*T*he next morning, Jack joined his new theater family at the Coral Cafe for breakfast. He and Leo sat at the chef's table in the kitchen, where Marina was making blueberry pancakes. Scout settled beside them, eagerly lifting his head or rolling over for anyone who wanted to pet him.

"Good morning, everyone," Jack said. "What a performance." In college, he had loved acting and writing. He hadn't had this much fun in a long time, and he was glad that Leo enjoyed it, too.

Ginger held a pot of coffee aloft. "Care for coffee, Jack?"

"Thanks, and I'll appreciate it if you keep that topped off for me." He pressed a hand to his forehead.

She smiled knowingly. "A little too much celebration last night?"

"I'm not used to that anymore," he said, grinning. Ginger sounded a little hoarse, too, and he recalled that

Bettina had been looking after her last night. "How is that cough this morning?"

"Still there, but I should be fine by the next performance," Ginger replied with her usual unshakable confidence.

Jack saw Marina frown, giving her grandmother a look of concern.

As Ginger moved on, Scout nudged Jack. Scratching his dog behind the ears, he surreptitiously checked his phone again. He wanted to find the critic's review of the play before anyone else to prepare them. It probably wouldn't be favorable.

What had he been thinking last night? That had been a fine way to destroy what little reputation he had left. He'd need that to find work in Zurich, where it was a lot more expensive to live than Summer Beach.

Yet, in his heart, Jack knew why he'd exploded on stage with that crazy skit. He wanted to shift the attention from Marina when she froze. She hadn't been in the spotlight since she'd left her position in San Francisco. And that final news show performance still embarrassed her. It wasn't her fault; she'd been set up, and the director should have cut away and gone to commercial.

Jack had been determined that Marina wouldn't be embarrassed again. These days, a lot of people filmed on mobile phones. She didn't need a part two disaster. Besides, Marina had recovered well on stage once she stopped taking herself so seriously. He was sure she'd be fine at the next show.

Even though Kai had been enthusiastic about his performance last night, Jack figured that was only because they'd managed to save the scene. In the clear light of morning, better judgment would surely prevail.

Leo spoke up beside him. "Can I have eggnog?"

"And how did you know there was eggnog in the refrigerator?" Ginger asked, tousling the boy's hair.

"It's on the chalkboard," Leo said, pointing to the new daily specials board that Marina had devised.

"Coming right up," Ginger said.

Across the table, Kai and Axe were talking about changes to the show, and Heather and Ethan were looking at photos of the show on their phones that friends had taken and sent them. Other cast and crew members were now spilling outside onto the patio, where Marina had set up a self-serve station with coffee and bagels. Everyone was anxiously awaiting Rexford's review that Carol said would be posted this morning. It had been Marina's idea that they all find out together over breakfast.

Jack tapped the screen. *Still nothing.*

"You're making me nervous by checking every ten seconds," Marina said.

He put the phone down. "I'll give it a rest."

She turned back to the stove and flipped the first pancakes onto a plate. "Who's the hungriest here?"

Leo shot up his hand, and everyone laughed.

"You snooze, you lose," Kai said. Rising from the table, she took the plate and placed it in front of Leo. "Who's next?"

Carol and her husband Hal appeared in the doorway, looking casual in their jogging gear. After greeting everyone, Carol blurted out, "Has Rexford posted his review yet?"

"I haven't really checked," Jack said, not wanting to seem too eager.

Kai laughed. "Not in the last ten seconds, that is."

"Keep checking," Carol said, sounding nervous.

Jack grinned and turned on his phone again. "Hey, the review just came in." He sat up and began reading it.

Carol jabbed him. "For heaven's sake, read it aloud."

"Here goes," Jack said, reading from the screen as everyone leaned in. "'Will *A Christmas Carol* ever be the same after a performance in Summer Beach? Substituting sandy shores for snowy climes, professional thespian Kai Moore lands in the Southland village for her debut directorial effort featuring Grammy Award-winner Carol Reston, known for hitting impossibly high notes.'"

Carol groaned and rolled her eyes at that. Jack wondered why, but he went on reading.

"'With uplifting musical numbers and a surprising holiday rap number performed by Pulitzer prize-winning journalist, Jack Ventana, *A Christmas Carol…At the Beach* is a sweet holiday show suitable for families. Now playing at the new Seashell outdoor amphitheater. Two thumbs-up for a rollicking good time.'"

A collective sigh of relief coursed through them, and Kai threw up her hands. "Whew, we survived the first review. But we couldn't have done it without a fabulous cast and crew."

Cheers went up across the patio. Carol seemed pleased for them, too. He figured she was a perfectionist, and at her level, she had to be. Carol was the headliner and main draw for the show.

Despite opening night jitters and errors, Jack knew everyone had done their best. Still, he recalled seeing Carol and Hal talking to the critic last night. He wondered if they had asked Rexford for a favor.

"That review is thanks to you," Kai said, hugging Carol.

Hal chuckled. "If you only knew. We were afraid Rexford would trash the show on account of Carol."

"Don't go telling stories," Carol said, swatting his arm.

Kai put her hands on her hips. "Now, you have to spill it."

"Oh, all right," Carol said. "You and everyone here earned that review on your own. Rexford has seldom given me a good review. He's a master of the back-handed compliment."

Jack looked at the review again. "But he wrote, 'known for hitting impossibly high notes.' Isn't that high praise?"

"Only on the surface," Carol said. "For years, he's been critical of my high notes. So, *impossibly* is the operative word. He says my opera training hurts his ears. I guess he has to create controversy for people to keep following his reviews."

"Therefore, he must have loved the show," Hal said, putting his arm around his wife. "That's all that matters to folks here in Summer Beach. People will be curious, and they'll come to see it. Rexford has a large following. I think he respected Jack's credentials—and his originality with that crazy scene. It was unexpected, so it was twice as funny."

"It was completely unintentional," Jack said, laughing. "We don't have to keep it."

"That scene absolutely stays in," Kai said. "We'll work on changes to the lyrics this afternoon. Will you join us?"

"I suppose so," Jack said, still feeling a little embarrassed. "As long as Leo and Scout can hang out here."

. . .

AFTER BRUNCH, Jack joined Kai and Axe in the cottage to revise lyrics for the new scene. Vanessa had dropped Leo off this morning, so Marina took the boy to help her in the garden.

While Kai and Axe made notes on Jack's scribbled lyrics, he watched Marina and Leo through the window. Leo seemed as excited to pull weeds as carrots.

With a sigh of resignation, Jack realized how much he would regret leaving Summer Beach. Yet, that seemed the only solution to support Leo. He wished he'd had more time with Marina. In retrospect, he should have acted on his feelings. However, that wouldn't have altered this present dilemma. Moving would have been that much harder.

Last night, Ginger had told him that he could continue working on her children's book illustrations in Switzerland, and he promised to return for working meetings. After the holidays, Jack would have to find another home for Scout, which he hated to do. He would also give up his beach cottage and look for a flat in Zurich. Although Jack had always liked visiting Switzerland, he sure would miss Summer Beach.

And most of all, Marina.

At least he was leaving her with Cole, who genuinely seemed to care for her. Jack bit his lip. He didn't like thinking of them together, but he wanted Marina to find happiness.

After they had finally gotten the lyrics the way they wanted them, Kai and Axe left to check on the other issues at the theater. Marina had already gone to open the cafe for supper, taking Leo with her. At his age, the boy was always hungry, and she had promised to make him something to eat.

Denise and John were returning for dinner at the Coral Cafe, and Jack knew Vanessa would be joining them and taking Leo home for school the next morning. After gathering his notes, Jack stepped outside the cottage to clear his head for a few minutes and let Scout out.

"All right, boy. Let's do this." Jack turned up the collar to his windbreaker.

Trotting ahead of him, Scout angled for the beach. In the distance, Jack could see people putting up decorations on their beach houses. Besides the holiday performance, he was also looking forward to the Santa Sprint—an annual beach run—and the holiday boat cruise. Bennett had invited him onto his boat this year. They would trim the boat with lights and cruise the coast with others. The entire marina would be a fun party scene.

Jack would miss the pleasures of Summer Beach. As he crested a dune, he saw Ginger walking toward him. She wore a jogging suit with a scarf tied around her neck.

"Out for a promenade?" Ginger asked.

"Scout's idea."

"Dogs keep you fit."

"Especially this one," Jack said, tossing a stick to Scout. "Would you like to join me? I'm not going far, and we can talk about ideas for the new illustrations."

They fell into step with each other and strolled along the water's edge, discussing their current story.

"I'll miss sharing thoughts with you in person," Ginger said, sliding her hand into the crook of his elbow.

"So will I," he said, letting Ginger latch onto his arm.

Not that she needed support, but they enjoyed a companionable stroll.

As they walked, Ginger said, "I've been thinking about your situation and how sad it will be for Leo to leave Summer Beach."

"I dread telling him." Yet, who was Jack to stand in the way of a boy's adventure? Leo might enjoy living in Europe, where so many opportunities awaited him. Considering the positives, he thought of how much his son could explore, from travel and culture to history, cuisine, and language. Jack enjoyed all that, too. But he would miss Summer Beach and their friends here.

Especially Marina.

Ginger pierced his thoughts. "Do you think Vanessa is acting too swiftly?"

"I'm hardly one to talk," he replied with a grin. "I've made snap decisions all my life."

"But not with Leo."

"Of course not."

"Perhaps you should have another heart-to-heart talk with Vanessa. Maybe there's another option—one you might not even know about."

"That would take a miracle, I'm afraid."

A slow smile spread across Ginger's face. "Some might say that about Vanessa's recovery. You see, we often underestimate the possibilities."

She angled her head toward the sea. "When we look out to the ocean, we can't see what lies beneath. Problems are like that, too. The solution might be floating just below the surface—or it might be glimmering in the depths—but until we break the surface, we won't know that possibilities even exist. You must dive for the answer or the best solutions." Pausing, she added, "From your profession, I know you're well versed in that."

He was, indeed. "I suppose I should apply those skills to my personal life." Jack glanced at Ginger, but she merely dipped her chin. If there was one lesson he'd learned from the Delavie-Moore clan and life in Summer Beach, it was to expect the unexpected. "I'll speak to Vanessa."

Patting his shoulder, Ginger said. "I don't want to see you lose hope. I believe there is always a way to be with the ones we love. Maybe not the most obvious way, but you're tenacious and creative."

Jack chuckled. "Why do I feel like you know me better than I know myself?"

Ginger gave him an enigmatic smile and started back toward the cottage.

20

"*H*ere's your tea," Marina said, placing a cup before her grandmother at the kitchen table.

The kitchen was fragrant from a batch of rosemary bread in the oven, and the sun cast warmth through the window. While the bread baked, Marina had simmered ginger root and added local honey to the brew.

Although Ginger's cough had improved, Marina was still concerned about the effect of the cool evenings on her grandmother. For as strong as Ginger was, she wasn't invincible. Fortunately, Ginger had rested during their days off, but the official opening night was tomorrow.

Marina eased into the chair beside her. "Your voice is sounding stronger."

"That's because of your good medicine here," Ginger said, raising her cup to take a sip. "The weather won't be as cold tomorrow night."

Marina chuckled at her grandmother's certainty. "Don't let the sunshine deceive you."

"Of course, I don't," Ginger said. "I spoke to my friend,

who is a scientist in meteorology. No chance of rain either —that has been my primary concern. But I could use another layer under my cape," Ginger said.

"That's a good idea. I'll do that, too."

"And a lovely wool scarf around my neck," Ginger added. "I have beautiful ones collected over the years. Bertrand used to spoil me on our travels, insisting that I have the finest Italian wool scarves to keep me warm. Did I ever tell you about our first winter in Paris when the heat went out?"

Marina smiled. Ginger was regaining her spirit. "It was Christmas, as I recall," Marina said. "I'll bet Kai will want to hear that story when she comes downstairs."

Ginger understood her subtle meaning. "Of course, you've heard it so many times. I'll save it for Kai."

"I'll ask Axe's crew to run an extension cord to plug in a small heater behind you during the show. That will keep you toasty."

"What a grand idea," Ginger said. "And I have another one. Since Leilani is cleared to return to the show—thank heavens her ankle had only a minor twist—I've decided to select you as my co-narrator. We could appear together, thus halving our speaking time. That would be easier on my throat. You're professionally trained, so I'm sure Kai will agree. My script is in the prop book; you can simply read as if you were on-air."

Marina considered the thought. "That reminds me of the play, *Love Letters*, where the actors read from correspondence exchanged over the years."

"Exactly," Ginger said. "How clever of Kai to write her script like that."

"We'll talk to Kai." Marina hoped her sister would be

amenable to the idea. She had planned to perform with Jack this week as needed until Leilani returned, and frankly, Marina would be relieved when she did. Facing Jack and feeling his embrace had been more than she was prepared to handle on opening night. Her heart could take only so much.

Her pragmatic side told her she needed to begin distancing herself from him before he left, but her emotional half wanted to spend as much time as possible with him.

Studying her, Ginger sipped her tea. "Cole shared his travel plans with me. Do you think he will return to Summer Beach afterward?"

Marina rested her chin on her hand. "Are you asking me if I want him to return?"

A smile played on Ginger's lips. "The thought crossed my mind. Since Jack is leaving."

"Didn't you suggest that I book a trip to Switzerland?"

"I'm only testing your strength of conviction."

Marina laughed. "I think I'm going to throw both those fish back in the sea."

"I wouldn't be so quick to do that," Ginger said with a glint in her eye. "You certainly don't have to toss them both back."

Marina peered at her. "And which one do you think I should hang on to?"

Ginger gave a noncommittal shrug. "I certainly couldn't say. But you might listen to your heart," she added, tapping Marina's chest.

"See? You don't know either." Laughing, Marina rose to check on the bread. As she pulled out two loaves, another thought struck her. She rested the loaf pans on a cooling rack. "I believe I need to make a phone call back east."

Calmly, Ginger sipped her tea. "That sounds like an important call to make."

"Possibly life-changing," Marina said.

"Admirable," Ginger said. "Now, if only we could find a Christmas miracle for you, too."

Marina smiled at the thought, however far-fetched it seemed.

UPSTAIRS in her old childhood bedroom, Marina stacked white cutwork pillows against the iron headboard. It was toasty on the sun-warmed second floor, so she cracked a window to let in ocean breezes before she sat down on the bed and tucked a vintage quilt around her.

Staring up at the coded symbols Ginger had painted on a border near the ceiling, Marina thought about their meaning.

Love always triumphs. True love is eternal.

Pondering her approach, Marina searched her contacts for the number she had called not too long ago. She dialed, and after the phone rang a few times, her friend answered it.

"Hi, Babs, it's Marina."

"Aren't you sweet to call again? I was just thinking of you. Cole has told me all about the holiday show."

Babs sounded happy to hear from her. That was a good sign. "And he told me you were thinking of flying out to see it."

Her friend laughed. "That was silly of me to mention

such a thing. I don't know what I was thinking. Honestly, I have so much to do to get ready for Christmas."

"I think it would be fun," Marina said. "You should book a flight right away. Although the nights are chilly, it's still sunny most days here, and much warmer than in New England. When are your children arriving for the holidays?"

"They're both spending Christmas with their boyfriends' families. I knew I'd have to share them someday, but I didn't know it would be so soon."

"Will you bring your husband?" Marina asked. She held her breath, hoping Babs wouldn't avoid the question this time.

Silence filled the line.

Finally, her friend sighed. "I was too embarrassed to say anything, but he left me several months ago for a younger version. I haven't even told the children. Every time they ask I say he's away on a business trip. He couldn't stand retirement, so he went back to work. That's where he met *her*, of course." She sighed. "I'll tell them after the new year."

"I'm so sorry to hear that," Marina said, yet that might be the opening she needed. "But all the more reason you should come. We have an open bedroom at my grandmother's cottage, or you can stay at my friend's beachside inn."

"Wouldn't it be awkward?"

Marina thought she heard Babs sniff. "What do you mean?"

"Cole went to Summer Beach to look you up. I know he's interested in you. The other night when I called, he went on and on about how spectacular you were in the show. I don't want to stand in the way of his happiness. Cole is a good man. Sometimes I think I made a mistake leaving him. But once I started complaining about him to my so-called friends, they egged me on until I finally pushed him out the door. The replacement model wasn't nearly as good as the original."

Marina thought about how Cole's face lit up when Babs called. "Do you ever wish you hadn't tried to trade him in?"

"We can't change the past, so there's no use crying about it," Babs replied, sidestepping the question. "But I am wiser, and today I choose my friends more carefully. I wish you and I hadn't lost touch. What fun the four of us used to have."

Babs reminisced for a few minutes, and when there was a lull in the conversation, Marina tried again. "I'm worried about Cole making that trip back east by himself."

"He's made the trip just fine before."

"I'm sure he has," Marina said. "But we're all older now, aren't we? If you were to come out here, the two of you could drive back together and look out for each other. That motorcoach is a beauty."

Her friend hesitated. "Knowing how he feels about you, I'd feel awkward."

"Babs, I could never take your place in his heart. I wouldn't even want to try. To be honest, there's someone else in my life, too."

Marina bit her lip. That wasn't exactly true, although she wished it were. Jack would probably meet someone in Zurich, and he'd forget about her. But Cole and Babs belonged together. It was clear that they missed each other; they simply didn't know how to take the first step. Marina wanted them to have a second chance, and the last thing she wanted was to insert herself between them.

"Really?" Babs asked, sounding hopeful.

Marina hurried on. "I wish you could have seen the look on his face when your call came through the other night after the show. He told me no one he dated ever compared to you. He said, 'they weren't Babs.'"

"He said that?"

"He did, and I'm sure he'd tell you the same thing." Marina paused. "We've been friends from the early days, and I'm being straight with you. If you've ever thought about reconciling with Cole, now is your chance. By the time you and Cole return to New England, you'll know whether your relationship is meant to be again. Why don't you fly in and surprise him after the show? He would be thrilled."

Another long silence ensued. Marina had given Babs everything she needed to take the first step, but she couldn't push her. She picked up a pillow and squeezed it. "Babs, are you still on the line?"

"I'm looking up flights on my computer," Babs replied, her voice filled with excitement. "I can't believe I'm doing this, but I can be there tomorrow on an early flight. Should I book it?"

"Take the leap," Marina said. Helping her old friends reunite felt like the right thing to do. And with a little holiday magic thrown in, it might just work.

If having companionship was all that mattered to Marina, she could have settled for Cole. But she would have been doing her friends—and herself—a great disservice.

She only hoped Cole would be as excited as they were.

21

*E*arly the next morning, Marina stood on stage as Kai and Jack blocked out scene changes. Leilani's doctor had approved her return to the show, though she had to take it easy.

"I can't dance around the table just yet," Leilani said. "Still, I can perch on a stool or a chair and clap while the family circles the table."

"That would work," Kai said. "Marina, would you work with Ginger on the narration? I want to hear it with both of you reading, sort of like a holiday parade coverage. Alternating parts, as if you're reading together. We'll practice that next, and if it sounds good, you can finish at home."

"We'll be the new anchor team," Marina said, laughing.

Jack joined them after he rehearsed the scene changes with Leilani, and Marina and Ginger ran through the narration. "The two of you sound good together," he said.

"We're a natural team," Ginger said, rising from her

stool to stretch. "I must speak to Axe about our lighting, though."

Marina watched her grandmother go. Ginger was up to something, although Marina wasn't sure what. She turned to Jack. "You and Leilani looked great up there."

"I'll miss you in that scene," Jack said. "We had a lot of fun, even though it wasn't planned."

"I'll never forget it," Marina said. There was a lot about Jack she wouldn't forget.

Kai approached, clapping her hands. "What a show we're going to have tonight. I suggest everyone leaves and rests before the show. This is our official opening night. Who's as excited as I am?"

"We are," Marina called out as all around the theater, cries and whoops echoed. She turned to Jack. "I have a lot to get ready for tonight. See you later?"

"You bet."

Marina hurried back to the Coral Cottage. She was expecting Babs this afternoon before the show, and she'd told her she could stay with them. Marina smiled to herself, imaging how surprised Cole would be. She hoped he would take this surprise the right way and not think she was meddling.

Once she arrived at the cottage, Marina didn't have long to wait for her old friend. A knock soon sounded at the door.

Babs held her arms wide. "Marina!"

Her friend had changed little over the past two decades. "I'm so glad you came. You must have been right behind me." They talked a little about the flight, but Babs could hardly wait to talk about Cole. She'd bought a new sweater in a fancy boutique at the airport.

"What do you think?" Babs asked as she pulled a deep violet angora sweater from a shopping bag. "It's so soft, and he always loved this color on me. But I didn't expect so much sunshine here. Do you think it's too warm to wear it?"

Marina laughed. "Since you're accustomed to real winter weather, that sweater might be too warm for you during the day. But you'll need it tonight after the sun sets. And the color is gorgeous with your auburn hair. Come backstage as soon as the show ends."

Marina prepared two mugs of hot chocolate with cinnamon sticks, and they went upstairs to her bedroom to talk. Sitting cross-legged on the bed together, sipping their cocoa and sharing stories, Marina felt as she had when she was a young military wife.

Babs grinned. "Remember how excited we used to get when Cole and Stan came home on leave? I feel like that now."

"Cole will be excited to see you."

"Do you think so? He won't think it's silly or impetuous of me?"

"I think he'll be flattered—and very grateful." If Marina still harbored any affection in her heart for Cole beyond friendship, seeing the hope in Babs' eyes would have confirmed her decision to let him go. Yet, she still felt nothing more for Cole than she ever had. She remembered what Cole had told her at Beaches about having lost the love of his life. Helping two old friends reignite their passion was worth far more to her.

They talked more until Babs yawned. "Must be jet lag from the time zone change. Maybe I should take a nap."

"An hour or two of sleep would refresh you," Marina said. "You'll want to look and feel your best."

While her friend was sleeping in Brooke's old room, Marina put on her makeup for the show. She would go with Ginger, and Babs would come later with Brooke, who was handling the picnic box collections at the cafe this afternoon.

As she swept blush across her cheeks, Marina thought about how Kai had been right. The show had come together—almost magically, or so it seemed from the outside.

And as usual, with a lot of hard work.

Ginger tapped on the door. "It's almost showtime."

"I'm ready," Marina said. She rose and hooked her arm through her grandmother's. "Let's break a leg tonight."

"PLACES, EVERYONE," Kai called out, pacing the backstage area.

Marina peeked out over the gathering audience. Babs had arrived, and she was sitting near the front. Once the stage lights went up, Cole wouldn't be able to see her.

Backstage, Ginger gripped Marina's hand. "Feeling confident?"

"You bet I am," Marina said. They each held a book; Jack had made two props to have one as a backup.

The music began, the lights went up, and as Marina and Ginger stepped on stage to their stools, the crowd applauded.

The magic had begun.

Marina felt good about tonight, even though she knew critics were in the crowd. This was a role she knew how to perform. She and Ginger had practiced, and the cast wasn't as jittery as they had been for the soft opening.

As the show progressed, everyone acted confidently and did not repeat mistakes made during the first performance. More than that, Marina noticed they were having a great time.

So was the audience. They hissed at Axe as Scrooge, applauded Leo as Tiny Tim, and went wild for Kai as the Ghost of Christmas Past. Carol brought down the house with her stellar performance as the Ghost of Christmas Present, and Marina thought she hit the high notes beautifully.

Jack and Leilani's scene was a crowd favorite, too. As Jack led the children in a conga line around the table, Leilani clapped from the safety of a chair. Right away, the audience began to clap with her.

At last, through the miracle of the holidays, Scrooge was redeemed. He joined his nephew Fred's holiday celebration, wishing everyone a very happy Christmas.

The audience cheered and whistled, and then, as bells jingled and *ho-ho-ho* rang out, the lights went up on Santa Claus while small children gasped in awe.

Marina's heart was full of gratitude for the efforts of her fellow cast members, crew, and musicians. They had enhanced the holidays for those in the audience—and made memories that none of them under the stars that evening would ever forget.

Finally, Marina and Ginger's narration came to a close. In unison, they called out, "And a very Merry Christmas to all."

After they closed their books, Ginger put her arm

around Marina, and they left the stage, waving to the audience.

Backstage, Kai had happy tears glistening in her eyes. "It's time for everyone to line up to take your bow. You were all magnificent!" She and Axe jogged among the cast, hitting high-fives and hugging them.

When they fell into a queue, Jack stepped in behind her.

"You were fabulous," he said.

"So were you and Leilani. And Leo." Marina smiled happily. The children were grouped together—Leo, Samantha, Logan, and Brooke's boys, among others.

"I don't know who had more fun—us or the audience."

"Both," Kai said as Axe wrapped his arm around her waist. "And that's the way it should be." She gazed up at him with more love in her eyes than Marina had ever seen.

"I think you have quite a career ahead of you as a director," Axe said, kissing Kai's cheek. "You're the most remarkable woman I've ever met."

Watching the exchange between them warmed Marina's heart. They were so well suited to one another.

After the main actors had taken their bows, Kai signaled for extras and everyone else. They gathered behind them, and the audience whistled and cheered for everyone.

Suddenly, a woman's voice rang out from the front row. "Give it up for Cole Beaufort! Whoop, whoop!"

Cole stepped from the rear and called out, "Babs, honey? Are you out there?" His face lit with hope.

Babs erupted with a squeal and began waving and blowing kisses to him.

Laughing, Marina looked at Ginger. "I guess she couldn't wait to go backstage."

"This is even better," Ginger said, gesturing toward

Cole, who was motioning at Babs and striding toward the steps that led to the stage.

Everyone began cheering them on, and through the pathway the audience made for her, Babs raced up the steps. "I couldn't wait to see you."

Cole caught her in his arms and whirled her around. Throwing his head back, he laughed and spun, and when they finally came to a rest, he gathered her in his arms. "I'm thrilled that you came."

Babs smiled at him with such joy on her face. "Merry Christmas, my love."

In response, Cole's eyes glowed with love, and he took her in his arms and kissed her.

"That's the way it's done, mate," one man yelled out. The audience clapped and cheered, and people began hugging and kissing their spouses, too.

"Our first miracle of Christmas," Ginger said to Marina with a wink. "Thanks to you."

Watching her old friends, Marina was hopeful for them. They'd found their way back to each other—with a bit of a nudge.

"Let's spread the love," Carol said, raising her mistletoe-trimmed hat. She held it aloft over Kai, although even on her tiptoes, she couldn't reach over Axe's head.

With a deep laugh, Axe took the hat from Carol. Holding it high, he kissed Kai. Then, his expression rapt with love, he clasped her hand and swiftly dropped to one knee.

"My dear madam director, would you do the honor of marrying me someday? I've loved you from the moment I heard you singing in the bathtub."

Kai squealed and flung her arms around him. "Yes, oh

yes! To paraphrase Jane Austen, a million, zillion times yes!"

Standing nearby, Marina laughed and clapped her hands. "Those two belong together," she said to her grandmother.

"It's the magic of Christmas," Ginger said. Smiling, she held up two fingers. "Our second miracle of the evening. And so well deserved."

Choking back tears of happiness, Kai turned to Marina and Ginger and reached out to them. A beautiful smile wreathed her face. Marina and Ginger joined them.

"When it's right, you know it," Marina whispered, and Kai nodded enthusiastically. This time, Kai had found her soulmate.

Friends gathered around Kai and Axe, congratulating them, and everyone was in high spirits.

After Marina hugged Kai, she felt a hand on her shoulder. Turning around, she faced Jack. As if it were the most natural thing to do, Marina closed her eyes and took a step toward him. He wrapped his arms around her, and their lips met as if long destined.

Lingering in his embrace, Marina let herself go, living in the moment. Everything about this felt so right as if they were right where they should be. She never wanted this feeling to end.

With reluctance, Jack pulled away. In a voice laden with emotion, he whispered, "Merry Christmas." And kissed her once again.

AFTER THE AUDIENCE THINNED, the cast and crew gathered backstage, still hugging and congratulating each other.

Marina stood chatting with her family and friends, and Jack and Leo stayed close beside her. She enjoyed the camaraderie that had developed among the cast and crew. Performing with Ginger was an enjoyable highlight of the holiday season that she would never forget.

As everyone picked up their belongings to leave, Marina said to Kai, "Will I see you later at the house?"

"Later," Kai said, her eyes still sparkling with love and excitement. "We have to meet some VIPs with Carol and Hal now."

Axe smiled at his new fiancée and took her hand. "Spirits & Vine is the closest place we have to Sardi's in New York. You should join us."

"Or maybe we can make the Coral Cafe the new post-theater hang-out," Kai suggested.

"Please, I have to sleep sometime," Marina said, laughing. "Besides, we don't have an alcohol license, and I expect champagne might be in your near future. You two have a lot to celebrate tonight."

Just then, Samantha called out, "Leo, your mom is here for you."

Jack hugged his son. "You did a great job tonight, kiddo. See you tomorrow after school."

"Thanks, Dad," Leo said. The boy turned and hurried toward his mother.

Vanessa stood beside Denise and John, who were picking up Samantha. There was a fourth person in their party Marina didn't recognize.

After hugging Leo and telling him how wonderful he'd been on stage, Vanessa straightened and gestured to a genial-looking man beside her. "Leo, I'd like you to meet

Dr. Noah Hess. He helped me get well, and he came from Switzerland to see you perform."

This slight, bespectacled man was the one who was whisking away Vanessa and Leo—and inadvertently, Jack. Marina expected him to look stern and demanding, but he seemed like a quiet, good-natured man with keen intelligence. Dr. Hess had not only helped save Vanessa's life with a remarkable treatment, but he'd also put a spark of love in her eyes.

Marina sighed. How could she fault them for such good fortune?

"Leo, I'm so pleased to meet you," Noah said, bending slightly and giving the boy a warm smile.

"Thanks for helping my mom. What did you think of the show?" Leo asked, his enthusiasm still bubbling over.

Noah smiled and patted Leo on the shoulder. "What a fine performance you gave. I think you have a real talent for the theater."

Leo beamed at Noah. They were clearly off to a good start, Marina thought.

"At least until Christmas," Vanessa said.

Had she heard correctly? Marina thought that Vanessa would be taking him out of the show early, right after school ended. They still had a few shows after that date.

"We have a surprise for you, Leo," Vanessa said, a smile lighting her eyes.

Marina sucked in a breath. She wished this could wait. Leo was having such a good time tonight, and she hated for news of their pending move to spoil that. Maybe Leo would be excited to move, but she didn't think so—not once he realized the move was permanent.

Beside her, Jack also seemed to sense what was coming.

He stepped to Leo's side and put his arm around his son. "I'm Jack, Leo's father." He held out his hand to Noah.

"I've heard a lot of good things about how devoted you are to Leo," Noah said, shaking his hand.

Vanessa bent to kiss Leo on the cheek. "I have wonderful news. Dr. Noah is moving to California. He's accepted an important position in Los Angeles, so we'll see a lot of him in Summer Beach."

Marina breathed out in relief. She could hardly believe what she'd heard, and Jack seemed speechless.

"Leo loves Summer Beach," Vanessa said softly to Jack. "And a lot of people here love him."

Squeezing his eyes against his sudden emotion, Jack wrapped his arms around his son. "Thank goodness," he whispered.

"Hey, Dad, too tight," Leo said, squirming and giggling. "Besides, I'm starving." Wresting free, he grabbed Samantha's hand, and the two kids dashed off toward the snack bar Marina had set up backstage.

"He's always famished," Vanessa said, laughing.

Jack hugged her and then shook Noah's hand again. "I'm so happy for both of you, and thank you from the bottom of my heart."

Noah inclined his head in appreciation and put his arm around Vanessa. "When Vanessa told me how happy Leo was in Summer Beach and what a good place it was for them to live, I decided to call my colleagues in Los Angeles. I've had an open offer to join them for some time, but I'd never had any other reason to be there." He gazed fondly at Vanessa.

"Now you do," Vanessa said, smiling. "I told you Leo's father would be pleased."

Turning back to Marina, Jack held his arms wide. "Can you believe it? We're staying!"

Marina could hardly believe what was happening. She clamped a hand over her mouth, half laughing, half crying.

Beside her, Ginger touched her shoulder and said softly, "Go to him."

Without hesitating, Marina stepped toward Jack, and he folded her into an embrace. In an instant, she felt the strength and intensity of his heartbeat match hers. Their unexpected relief was mutual.

"This is a miracle," Jack said, his voice husky with emotion. "I hope this will change things between us, too."

"It already has," Marina said, feeling the love she'd suppressed growing in her heart. "Let's start over, Jack."

He shook his head. "Everything we've gone through has made us stronger. Let's start from where we are and build *us* better."

Glancing over Jack's shoulder, Marina saw Ginger standing to one side. With a smile, her grandmother raised three fingers, kissed them, and blew Marina a kiss.

"This is a true miracle of Christmas," Marina said, nestling her cheek against Jack's.

LATER, as the cast members were gathering their belongings to leave, Jack asked, "Would you like to walk to the village? We can talk along the way and meet Kai and Axe at Sprits & Vine."

"I'd like that," Marina said, eager to be alone with him before joining the others. "Ginger can take the car home."

As they walked, Marina tucked her hand through the crook in his elbow. She detected the sweet scent of burning fireplaces on the crisp sea breezes. Shop windows gleamed with holiday decorations, and palm trees wrapped with tiny white lights rustled in the light breeze. The aroma of pine and fir rose on the night air.

"The holidays are magical at the beach," Jack said. "I can't wait to see the surfing Santas I've heard about."

"It's an old annual tradition," Marina said, laughing. "Leo will love that. I'm so happy he and Vanessa are staying here for Christmas."

Jack put his arm around her. "Would you go out to dinner with me next week? The theater is dark on Tuesday, or we could have a later dinner on Saturday after the show."

"Are you asking me out on a date?" Marina said, teasing him.

"I sure am."

"Be careful; it could cost you."

"I'm not worried." Jack grinned. "I had a bet at Java Beach that paid off handsomely, so I'm flush with cash right now. Let's go have a good time."

Marina arched an eyebrow. "That wouldn't be the wager that involved me, would it?"

"I've learned to always bet on myself," Jack said, winking. "Even when I'm the long shot, which I was for quite a while."

At that, she threw back her head and laughed. "You didn't."

Jack shook his head. "But seriously, I've made reservations at Beaches for us—without Scout this time. I don't think he's welcome there anymore. Which date would you like?"

Not wanting to appear too eager, Marina folded her

arms. Besides, he deserved this. "I don't know. What else do you have in your bag of choices?"

Jack rubbed his forehead. "How about a dinner cruise on the water?"

Wrinkling her nose, Marina shook her head. "Too many tourists."

"Guess I need to step up my game. Okay, here goes." Jack blew out a breath. "Hal offered to fly us to Los Angeles on his private plane for a fancy dinner sometime. He invited us to go with them, or his pilot can take us."

Marina drummed her fingers, enjoying this. "Maybe something that doesn't involve aerial or aquatic transportation."

"Sure." He passed a hand over his chin. "There's always my trusty Volkswagen van, Rocinante. It's good on land."

"I see. We're getting somewhere with the Don Quixote reference." She pressed her lips together to keep from laughing. At this point, she didn't care where they went, just that they were together.

After some soul searching, Marina had questioned why it meant so much to her that Jack make good on his promise of asking her out, when what was more important were the challenges they faced together and the support they shared. She'd been looking for proof that he cared, but she had overlooked important signs.

Jack had proven himself during the show. He'd risked making a fool of himself and damaging his professional reputation to save her embarrassment. She saw the kind of man he was in his thoughtful consideration of everyone from Leo and Vanessa to Ginger and others in Summer

Beach. He'd professed his love for Marina, but more than that, his actions confirmed it.

Jack grinned. "I'm planning to decorate the old van for the holidays. How about you, me, Rocinante, and Rosa's tacos on the beach?"

"Any day you want, Mr. Cratchit."

In front of the twinkling lights on Main Street, Jack clasped Marina's hand to his heart. "You'll always be my Mrs. Cratchit."

"Are these our new nicknames?" Marina asked, laughing.

"I can think of better ones that are more us," Jack said, tracing her fingers. "And that's a promise I intend to keep. Just so you know."

Questions swirled through her mind, yet Marina raised her lips to his. "Are you sure about that?"

"Never surer." Jack's lips touched hers. "Merry Christmas, Mrs. Cratchit, but I'd rather say Ventana."

Hearing that warmed Marina's heart. Although they weren't ready for such a big step, she liked that they were moving in that direction. "You keep betting on yourself," she began playfully. "And if you're lucky, you might get to say that someday."

"I'd like that very much," Jack said, lifting a strand of hair from her face and smoothing it from her forehead with a gentle hand. "What I want is a life together—you, me, and all our wonderful kids, small and large."

Marina liked that he included Heather and Ethan along with Leo. "Don't forget Scout."

"How could I?" Jack chuckled. "That nutty dog brought us together on more than one occasion."

Laughing, they stopped in front of the colorful lights at the door to Spirits & Vine. Looking up, Marina spied the classic holiday greenery above them. She slid her arms around Jack's neck, threading her fingers through the nape of his thick hair. This was the man she wanted in her life, too. Not only for the holidays but every day after that. "Merry Christmas, Jack."

"And many, many more," he said, kissing her under the mistletoe.

AFTERWORD

Author's Note:

Thank you for reading *Coral Holiday*, and I hope you enjoyed the debut of the new Seashell theater. If you'd like to see what happens next, join me in *Coral Weddings* for more heartwarming fun. While Marina and Jack contemplate next steps, Kai plans a surprising wedding to Axe.

If you've read the *Seabreeze Inn* at Summer Beach series, you're also invited to welcome a new baby in *Seabreeze Shores*, the next in that series.

Keep up with my new releases and new series on my website at JanMoran.com. Please join my Reader's Club there to receive news about special deals and other goodies.

More to Enjoy

If this is your first book in the Coral Cottage series, be sure to meet Marina when she first arrives in Summer Beach in *Coral Cottage*. If you haven't read the Seabreeze Inn at Summer Beach series, I invite you to meet art teacher Ivy Bay and her sister Shelly as they renovate a historic beach house in *Seabreeze Inn*, the first in the original Summer Beach series.

You might also enjoy more sunshine and international travel with a group of friends in the *Love California* series, beginning with *Flawless* and an exciting trip to Paris.

Finally, I invite you to read my standalone historical novels, including *Hepburn's Necklace* and *The Chocolatier*, a pair of 1950s sagas set in gorgeous Italy.

Most of my books are available in ebook, paperback or hardcover, audiobooks, and large print. And as always, I wish you happy reading!

CORAL HOLIDAY RECIPES

As I write, I often immerse myself into my fictional world with music, food, and other elements in the story. For *Coral Holiday*, I mined recipes I've made over the years for Christmas, Hanukkah, New Year's Day, ski trips, and other wintry celebrations with friends and family. I could just imagine Marina serving these at the Coral Cafe by the beach.

In making recipes, I often tweak them to create healthier alternatives for those with dietary restrictions, so feel free to experiment. I prepare many gluten-free and reduced-sugar options for my family and friends.

I hope you'll enjoy these, but most of all, enjoy your time with cherished loved ones during the holiday season—and any time of year.

Cranberry-Orange Holiday Muffins

2 cups flour
3/4 cup sugar (or sugar alternative)
2 teaspoons baking powder
1/2 teaspoon salt
1 egg
2/3 cup plain or Greek yogurt, or 2/3 cup milk
1/4 cup orange juice
1/2 cup oil (vegetable, avocado, canola oil, or other light oil)
1 teaspoon grated orange zest or to taste
1-1/2 cups cranberries, fresh or frozen (drained)
Optional: 1/4 cup chopped nuts, i.e., macadamia, pecans

Preheat oven to 400 F.
1. Combine dry ingredients in a large bowl.
2. In the same bowl, add and stir in wet ingredients, mixing just until moistened.
3. Fold in orange zest and cranberries.
4. Pour into a silicone muffin tray or greased muffin tin.
Top with streusel mixture if desired (below).

Bake at 400 F for 20 to 25 minutes (for jumbo muffins) or until a knife or toothpick comes out clean. For medium muffins, bake 15 to 20 minutes. For mini-muffins, bake 10 to 12 minutes. (Tip: Set your timer for a couple of minutes early in case your oven temperature varies.)

Gluten-free version: In place of flour, use 1 cup almond flour and 1 cup coconut flour (or other as desired), and 1 egg. Or, use a simple all-in-one blend such as Cup4Cup Gluten-Free

Flour, King Arthur Gluten-Free Measure for Measure
Flour, or Bob's Red Mills Gluten-Free 1-to-1 Baking Flour.

Easy Streusel Topping (Optional)

1-1/4 cups flour
1/3 cup packed light or dark brown sugar (or sugar
alternative)
1/3 cup white sugar (or sugar alternative)
1/4 teaspoon salt (omit if using salted butter)
1 teaspoon cinnamon
1/2 teaspoon nutmeg
1/2 cup unsalted butter, melted
1/2 teaspoon extract
Optional: 1/4 cup chopped nuts, i.e., macadamia, pecans

1. Mix flour, sugar, salt if desired, and dry spices.
2. Melt and cool butter. If the butter is too hot, it will melt
the sugar and not be crumbly.
3. Pour butter over the mixture and fold in just until
crumbly. Clumps are okay and desired. Do not over mix.
4. Sprinkle crumb mixture over muffins before baking.

If baking muffins with streusel topping, muffins may need a
little longer baking time.

Gluten-free version: In place of flour, use 1 1/4 combined
almond flour and coconut or rice flour (or other as desired).
Or use an all-in-one blend, such as Cup4Cup Gluten-Free
Flour, King Arthur Gluten-Free Measure for Measure
Flour, or Bob's Red Mills Gluten-Free 1-to-1 Baking Flour.

Classic Hot Buttered Rum

For the spiced batter (makes 4 drinks):

1/3 cup salted butter, softened
3 tablespoons dark brown sugar
1 teaspoon cinnamon
1/2 teaspoon nutmeg
1/4 teaspoon allspice

For each drink:

1-1/2 tablespoons of spiced batter
2 ounces dark rum or 2 ounces of apple cider or apple juice
6 ounces boiling water
Optional: cinnamon stick or sliced orange

1. Scoop spiced batter into a mug.
2. Pour boiling water over and stir.
3. Add dark rum to taste.
4. Garnish with a cinnamon stick or sliced orange

This batter freezes well, so you can double or triple recipe and store in a resealable container. Scoop out as needed. (And please drink responsibly.)

For a nonalcoholic version, substitute apple cider or apple juice for the rum. If you like a rich apple flavor, use apple cider or juice in place of water, too. To create a creamier consistency, add a splash of half-and-half or creamer. You may also use a sugar alternative or reduce the sugar.

ABOUT THE AUTHOR

JAN MORAN is a *USA Today* bestselling author of romantic women's fiction. A few of her favorite things include a fine cup of coffee, dark chocolate, fresh flowers, laughter, and music that touches her soul. She loves to travel, and her favorite places for inspiration are those rich with history and mystery and set against snowy mountains, palm-treed beaches, or sparkly city lights. Jan is originally from Austin, Texas, and a trace of a drawl still survives, although she has lived in Southern California for years.

Most of her books are available as audiobooks, and her historical fiction is translated into German, Italian, Polish, Dutch, Turkish, Russian, Bulgarian, Portuguese, and Lithuanian, and other languages.

Visit Jan at JanMoran.com. If you enjoyed this book, please consider leaving a brief review online for your fellow readers where you purchased this book, or on Goodreads or Bookbub.

Made in United States
North Haven, CT
05 November 2022

26338902R00139